HOME TRUTHS

Jill MacLean
HOME TRUTHS

DANCING CAT  BOOKS

The publisher gratefully acknowledges the support of the Canada Council for the Arts
and the Ontario Arts Council for its publishing program.
We acknowledge the financial support of the Government of Canada
through the Canada Book Fund for our publishing activities.

 Canada Council **Conseil des Arts**
for the Arts **du Canada**

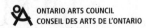 **ONTARIO ARTS COUNCIL**
CONSEIL DES ARTS DE L'ONTARIO

Library and Archives Canada Cataloguing in Publication

MacLean, Jill
Home truths / Jill MacLean.

ISBN 978-1-897151-96-9

1. Abused children—Juvenile fiction. I. Title.

PS8575.L415H64 2010   jC813'.6   C2010-904417-7

U.S. Publisher Cataloging-in-Publication Data
(Library of Congress Standards)
United States Library of Congress Control Number: 2010931059
MacLean, Jill.
Home truths / Jill MacLean.
[   ] p. : cm.
Summary: Brick's plan to escape an abusive father is derailed when he discovers that his
little sister is no longer safe and will need her big brother's protection until they are
both old enough to leave home. But Brick is a bully too, and he will have to
make amends before finding some unexpected allies.
ISBN-13: 978-1-897151-96-9

1. Abused children — Juvenile fiction. 2. Bullying — Juvenile fiction.
3. Fathers and sons — Juvenile fiction. 4. Brothers and sisters — Juvenile fiction. I. Title.
[Fic] dc22   PZ7.M3454Hom 2010   LCCN: 16295011

NOVA SCOTIA
Tourism, Culture and Heritage

The author is grateful for financial support from the Province of
Nova Scotia through the Grants to Individuals Program of the
Department of Tourism, Culture & Heritage. The Author wishes
to acknowledge the support of the Canada Council for the Arts
through the Grants to Professional Writers Program.

Cover design and image by Angel Guerra/Archetype
Interior text design: Tannice Goddard, Soul Oasis Networking

Manufactured by Transcontinental Gagné, with 100% post-consumer waste recycled paper
in Louisville, Quebec, Canada in August 2010. Job# 41210.

Dancing Cat Books
An imprint of Cormorant Books Inc.
215 Spadina Avenue, Studio 230, Toronto, Ontario, Canada M5T 2C7
2250 Military Trail, Tonawanda, New York, USA 14150
www.dancingcatbooks.com • www.cormorantbooks.com

FSC
Mixed Sources
Product group from well-managed
forests, controlled sources and
recycled wood or fiber

Cert no. SW-COC-000952
www.fsc.org
© 1996 Forest Stewardship Council

For Barbara and MoJo,
who hold so many of my stories

1.1 [close to the bone]

LIGHTS FLASH, my score pops up—best ever—and the game's over. I played *Rescue 911* first, then *Buck Hunter*, got right into it, hands and brain working together. A real buzz.

I shrug into my hoodie and saunter out of the arcade like I own the place. At Subway, I check out the menu. After I've returned the library books, the plan is to come back here and eat in one of the booths, a Footlong Cold Cut Combo, extra mustard and onion, skip the tomato.

I wander around The Source, looking at all the electronic stuff I don't have, then head for the mall exit. Lorne Meisner is standing outside the beauty parlor, his back to me, waiting for his mom. Any other eleven-year-old would be in the arcade or the sports store. Not Lorne. He's such a jerk, just about begs you to pick on him.

Can't give him a wedgie at the mall.

My sneakers quiet on the tile floor, I amble up behind him, dig my fingers deep into his shoulder, and squeeze. The kid's nothing but bone and gristle.

I say, innocent as can be, "Hey, Lorne. How's it going?"

"Good." He's trembling.

"Only good?" I squeeze a little harder.

"Real good." He starts whimpering, so I let go.

He scuttles into the beauty parlor.

When I turn around, a jolt goes right through me. Pete MacLellan, Floyd's boss, five-feet-seven in his built-up heels, is stationed near the pet store, staring at me. He was brought in from Truro a year ago, after the previous manager retired. Ever since, it's been no fun living with Floyd, who'd obviously assumed he'd be the next boss.

Floyd is my father.

As I pass Pete, I nod politely. Then I aim for the exit, trying to walk the way Floyd walks, like you've got the world by the tail and you're whipping it around your head.

I cross the parking lot to Main Street. The GM dealership, where Floyd works, is on my left; I walk faster. The RCMP detachment is next, and the bakery. You can smell their chocolate chip cookies a block away. Why all the cops aren't overweight, I don't know.

The library is a red brick building with a few scrubby bushes on either side of the door. There's a rack just inside where they display the theme of the week. Perennial Gardening. No use to me.

Billy Gottrich is thumbing through the DVDs, the cuffs of his jeans bunched around his ankles, crotch mid-thigh. Pathetic. While it's tempting to hassle him, I decided long ago to keep my nose clean at the library.

After making sure he's not watching, I choose six picture books for Cassie, my little sister. They're all by Dr. Seuss, who's the flavor-of-the-month.

Three books have come in for me, travel books on the High Arctic and Mongolia, and an autobiography, as well as a couple of CDs: Metallica and AC/DC. The real bonus is a DVD of one of AC/DC's concerts. I swipe everything through the automatic checkout.

Let's get this over with. I'm a reader. Nonfiction mostly, because I like to hoard information. I've tried novels, but you can't trust the facts any more than you can trust the authors to keep the emotional lid on. I've even tried poetry. Lids off and toss 'em in the air, that's what poetry's all about.

Although I own an old-fashioned boom box with a CD player and an AM/FM radio, I don't own a laptop, iPod, iPhone, or Blackberry, and Floyd hogs the TV—what else is there to do every evening from November to April except read?

I wish I owned a laptop. On Sunday mornings, when he and Opal sleep in, I sneak into his study and use his; ditto when they go out together. But it's not as good as having your own.

1.2 [and introducing ...]

I'M WONDERING which book I'll start first, so my mind's somewhere else as I leave Main Street and cross behind a row of new Chevy Cobalts.

"Why aren't you home?"

I stop dead, like I'm the buck who's been shot.

Floyd strolls toward me in his blue striped shirt, freshly ironed, and his dark blue tie. You could slice an artery on the creases in his trousers.

"Did you hear me?" he says.

"I've just been to the library. I'm gonna grab a Sub, then I'll go home."

"Where did you get the money for a Sub?"

"Opal gave it to me." Opal's my mother.

When I left the house, she was upstairs in her office—the

place where she keeps her angel cards, crystals, and aromatherapy crap—so I helped myself from the jar in the pantry. Near enough to the truth, even for him.

Anyway, what can he do so close to the GM dealership? It's been nearly three weeks, though—twenty days, to be exact, and his max is usually a month. For some of that time he was on vacation, so I'm hoping it doesn't count.

"You can give the money back to her, kiddo, because you won't have time for lunch," Floyd says with that empty smile of his. "Two cords of hardwood are being delivered this morning."

"I'll go home right after I eat. It's only eleven o'clock."

He pulls my left wrist toward him, smiling nonstop, then pushes my sleeve up and twists my wrist as though he wants to check my watch. His nails bite into my skin. My watch strap's loose, which gives him the excuse to keep twisting until he can see the numbers. Pain shoots up my arm. I lower my shoulder, trying not to flinch, clinging to the books and CDs in my other hand.

"I'll go home right now."

He drops my arm. "Good," he says. "I'd better go back to work."

He strides between two of the Cobalts and disappears inside the glass doors of the showroom. Rubbing my wrist, I scuttle behind a big black truck. GMC Canyon. If I'd been paying attention, I could have avoided him.

1.3 [half-split]

THE ATV is parked behind Sobeys. I jam my hair under my helmet, not easy because it's long and thick, and buckle up. Floyd has his hair trimmed every three weeks by a barber who used to be in the military.

The mall backs onto Dave Sanger's woodlot; a network of trails through the trees around Hilchey Bay connects the houses, the river, and the logging roads. To go home, I follow the river upstream as far as the bridge. We had the wettest June in years, so what with mud and the usual rocks, steering takes concentration plus four-wheel drive.

Our place is near the bridge; Floyd inherited the house and all the furniture from his father before I was born. You can't see the house from the road because of the forest and because the driveway curves around some granite boulders. Erratics, left by the glaciers 10,000 years ago when the granite was already 370 million years old. Does this reduce Floyd to size? I wish.

Just as well the house doesn't show from the road because it's in serious need of a coat of paint and a new roof. Trees crowd around it as if they're propping it up.

I take the last bend, gravel spitting from under the tires, and jam the brakes on without even thinking about it. The ATV slews toward the ditch. To one side of Opal's car two cords of split hardwood have been dumped on the ground.

He did warn me.

Jeez, I'm not psyched for this. It happens once a year, and once a year it's my job to turn the heap into a woodpile. You've heard of obedience training? I'm the beagle.

I'll start after lunch, even though I won't do it right. Beats being accused of slacking off.

Before I can wipe the frown off my face, Opal comes out the side door, a handwoven bag slung over her shoulder. She's wearing her work clothes—long flowered skirt, fringed turquoise shawl, dangly earrings made of crystal. Her eyes are turquoise too, and it's not contacts. Cassie's are the same color, except Cassie's don't come at you like lasers.

Opal has straight black hair and cheekbones that'll stay put until she's ninety. It weirds me out that my own mother, no matter that she's piss-poor at the job, is beautiful.

"You were gone long enough," she says. "Cassie's inside."

"I want you to look after her again in a couple days."

"You don't run my life, Brick."

"You don't pay me for babysitting!" She and Floyd were

away last week. Seven whole days of Cassie, no time off for good behavior.

"We put a roof over your head."

"Some roof—covered in moss with the gutters falling off."

"Exactly," she says, with her feral smile. "I can't possibly bring my clients here, which is why I need you to babysit. I'll be back by four."

She's a psychic healer. Self-proclaimed.

She brushes past me and climbs into her shiny new Malibu. Three years ago when Floyd won the provincial award for GM Salesman of the Year, he and Opal went to Halifax for the ceremony. I can't remember ever calling them Mom and Dad. Or Mother and Father. I don't call Floyd anything, while Opal always made it clear that being anyone's mom was rock bottom on her list of priorities.

This seems like as good a time as any to deal with the basics:

Name:	Brickson (Brick) Thaddeus MacAvoy.
Father:	Floyd Thaddeus MacAvoy. Thaddeus was Floyd's father, who, by all reports, wasn't someone you'd want sitting across from you at the kitchen table. As for my name, the -son got dropped a long time ago.
Mother:	Opal MacAvoy, formerly Audrey Brickson —last name was dumped after Floyd swaggered into view, no regrets that I can see, and what kind of a name is

Audrey when you're preaching how a bunch of gardenias will bring about . universal love.

Sister: Cassandra (Cassie) MacAvoy, just turned four.

Age: fourteen years and seven months.

Grade: nine, next September (school's only been out a week and a half and already I'm bored out of my skull).

Sports: hockey, Bantam, B team, defense.

ATV: red Honda FourTrax Automatic that Floyd won at the hospital fundraiser (he doesn't like getting his clothes dirty, so he never goes near it. I'm allowed to use it, important errands only).

Girlfriends: none.

Address: 138 Hilchey River Road, RR #4, and no, I don't blame you if you've never heard of it. Head down the Eastern Shore of Nova Scotia and you're going in the right direction.

Nearest town: Hilchey Bay. Could be you've never heard of that, either.

Long-term plan: leave here the day I turn sixteen. Three weeks before Christmas. Yes, Floyd, there is a Santa Claus.

I WALK indoors, hang my helmet and hoodie in the mudroom, and go into the kitchen. Cassie's sitting at the table with her stuffed skunk. She calls him Rover because she wants a puppy, even though I told her we can't have one. Ever.

She's scowling at me. "You went to the library without me."

"You were asleep."

She shoves a picture book across the table. "We gotta take this back."

The book is about a pink dragon called Petronella, whose hobby is turning the villagers' gardens to soot. "It's not due yet."

"It gives me nightscares." That's her word for bad dreams.

"We'll take it back in a couple of days."

"Now!"

"We can't. I've got to do the woodpile. What was the night-scare about?"

"A dragon burned down all our trees. Its eyes were red like its brain was on fire. I hid under my bed and its claws went scritch-scratch on the floor."

"Gross."

"You weren't there to save me."

I pat her on the sleeve. "Dragons like Petronella live in far-away countries."

"She lives in our oven. She's why the tuna melts went black."

I had my nose stuck in a book and forgot about the tuna melts, that's why they went black. Try telling that to Cassie, who has enough imagination for six kids. Good thing she watches daytime TV. Tyrone and Pablo from *The Backyardigans* are sweeter than fudge, and so are the reruns of *Blue's Clues*.

"How about I make bacon and eggs for lunch?" I say.

"Then we'll go to the library."

"Not today, we won't. But I'll hide the book in my room so you'll be safe from Petronella."

"Ketchup on the eggs."

"Okay."

Floyd's empty coffee mug is still sitting on the table, the Eric Lindros mug he's had for years: Philadelphia Flyers, #88, good-looking guy, big, physical. Everything I'm not.

Sure, I'm tall for my age. But the day muscles were parceled out, I must have called in absent.

Using both hands—*you dropped it, kiddo?*—I place the mug in the dishwasher, back right-hand corner, nothing touching it. Then I fry up some bacon while Cassie watches for the toast to pop up. The bacon turns out crisp but not burnt, *perfecto* when you add eggs easy-over and toast slathered with strawberry jam. Cassie feeds the crusts to Rover.

Normally, with Floyd at work and Opal out, we could watch TV. I go upstairs, drag on my oldest jeans, and rummage for my work gloves in the bottom drawer. Floyd's the Hilchey River Road Woodpile Expert, studying the different types of wood and reading articles on the Internet. In the meantime, I supply the boy power because—let's not kid ourselves—manpower it ain't.

Manpower, I've decided, is like the peak of Everest. Not many get there and they leave a megatrail of garbage along the way. Useful Fact: if you're ever crazy enough to climb Mount Everest, in the Dead Zone at the peak where the oxygen runs out, you'll be staggering past the corpses of long-dead climbers. Impossible to cart them away. Don't get too big for your crampons.

Anyway, feel free to skip the following description of the MacAvoy Woodpile, as stacked by yours truly last July. It's behind the house in the middle of the clearing. It's two tiers deep, oriented west-east to catch the prevailing winds, the top covered with a black tarp (maximum heat absorption, hence maximum evaporation, up to fifty percent of the weight of green wood is water—I could go on). The whole thing sits on wooden pallets from Home Hardware. No bottom rot in our woodpile, no sir.

I lug six pallets from the cellar. First decision, where should they go? Don't want them under the trees. They shouldn't go too close to the back of the garage. Should I start by taking wood from last year's pile and stacking it in the cellar?

Should I lie down on the grass, put my ball cap over my eyes, and go to sleep?

After I lay the pallets on the far side of the present pile, I tip several wheelbarrow loads of wood onto the grass beside them. Birch logs, half-split, the grain pale. Put 'em bark side up, leave gaps for air circulation, one-over-two then two-over-one. I quit on the third row. I've shown willing without doing so much it'll take me all day tomorrow to redo it.

1.4 [the Semple challenge]

CASSIE'S WATCHING *Treehouse* when Opal gets home. Floyd won't be back for another hour and a half, and I'm in a lousy mood. I sneak out the side door, tramp down the driveway, and cross the road by the bridge. It's one of those days to plunk myself on a rock beside the river and blot everything out.

Today, it doesn't work. Two cords of wood. Bruises on my wrist. Thirty-one days in July. Thirty-one more in August. Cassie and me. Me and Floyd.

The river's so freaking goal-oriented, always on a big tear to reach the sea.

Eventually I stand up, wincing because the granite's rough and I don't have much in the way of padding. I'd better hike home. It would be just like Floyd to skip out early.

Then, as I clamber up the bank to the road, I get lucky.

Glenn Semple's walking across the bridge, his greyhound, Igor, ahead of him. No one else on the road owns a dog; but if they did, it'd be chained up, not mincing along on a pale blue leash that's long enough for six dogs.

Although Glenn's half a head shorter than me, he never has the wit to act scared. But I'm surprised Igor hasn't run for cover, seeing as how I've been known to fire rocks in his direction.

The leash is trailing in the dirt between me and Glenn. I don't want to get tangled in it, so I give Igor a kick in the ribs.

The dog yelps, skitters behind Glenn, and flattens himself against his legs.

Glenn bunches his fists. "You leave my dog alone!"

Before I can duck, he lands two good ones to my chest. I move in for the kill. "Dog? That's not a dog, it's an overgrown weasel."

My heels digging into the dirt, I grab his wrist, lever his arm behind his back, and pull up, nice and easy.

He's standing on tiptoes. His teeth are gritted, but he can't keep the sounds from escaping. He doesn't cry, though. Never has.

Igor whines in sympathy. Then I hear a logging truck at the top of the hill, jake brakes blatting as it starts down the slope to the bridge. I kick Glenn's feet from under him and let go of his arm. He drops to the ground, still clutching the leash. I'm halfway down our driveway before the truck roars past.

You gotta be careful with the arm-twisting routine because you can dislocate someone's shoulder that way. I googled it.

Glenn moved here from Toronto two years ago. His father is a retired music professor who owns a bookstore on Main Street. Glenn has blond curly hair, makes top marks in school, and plays the flute. He doesn't play hockey, football, basketball, or soccer. All of which should put him at the bottom of the social pile.

The girls are all over him. The guys like him. Even the jocks tolerate him.

None too smart putting *life* and *fair* in the same sentence.

1.5 [Brickpower]

FLOYD ARRIVES home at five thirty sharp. He brakes by the heap of birch logs and turns off the ignition of his Hummer H2 SUV, Silver Ice Metallic. He'll keep that vehicle until it's an antique.

I'm in the kitchen washing a saucepan. KD for supper, spirals at Cassie's request. Floyd walks around the logs then strolls out back. I fight the temptation to go to the other window and watch him.

Five minutes later he saunters into the kitchen and leans against the doorframe, hipshot. "Why did you put the pallets there?" he says, pleasantly enough.

"So last year's wood is nearest the cellar door?" Declarative statements can be dangerous. They don't teach you this in grade eight English.

"I keep hoping—against all the evidence—that you'll develop a modicum of brains and initiative. Wouldn't it have made more sense to start by piling last year's wood in the cellar?"

"Guess so."

"You guess so?"

"Yes. Yes, it would have made more sense."

"Do it, then. Correctly this time."

He pauses. My turn to say something. "Okay."

"Which pallets will you use?"

Trick question? "The ones I put on the grass?"

"Brilliant." He straightens. I tense. He says, "I expect the new wood to be stacked by the time I get home from work tomorrow. That's not asking too much, is it?"

I shake my head. Beagle with its tail between its legs.

"Once you're done in the dishpan, you'd better head for the cellar."

I nod. *Yes sir, yes sir, three bags full.* Which, in case your childhood was deprived of nursery rhymes, comes from "Baa, Baa, Black Sheep." After Cassie outgrew Mother Goose, she latched onto *Jack and the Beanstalk*, and if you're reading that book to a kid you don't have a worry in the world about TV violence.

The cellar isn't deep enough for me to stand up straight. The overhead light is a bare bulb, the steps rough wood, ending near a cupboard barricaded by boxes. The rest of the cellar? Cracked cement floor, cobwebs, grimy little windows—perfect set for a horror flick.

Our oil-wood furnace is state-of-the-art.

I haul open the door to the outside and toss the logs I piled this afternoon off the pallets. My wrist hurts. When I've carried the pallets back down to the cellar and lined them up a foot away from the side wall, I start transferring last year's dry wood into the cellar and stacking it just so.

I quit at a quarter to ten. Too dark outside to see what I'm doing, bumped my head twice on the sill, moths dashing themselves against the lightbulb, and I'm bone tired.

Wales is losing to the New Zealand All Blacks, so that takes care of Floyd. He prefers rugby to American football—no padding, more injuries. In my socked feet I circle his chair and climb the stairs. Cassie's fast asleep, Rover squashed against her chest, *Horton Hatches the Egg* lying open on the quilt. Usually I read her a bedtime story.

I set my alarm then read about the Gobi Desert of Mongolia. All that space with hardly anyone in it. Growing in the sand is a tree called saxaul, which camels like to eat. If you burn a saxaul tree, it gives off three times the heat of birch.

Long way to go for a cord of wood.

THREE IN the afternoon, twenty-seven degrees and not a breath of wind, the scorched smell of pine resin hangs in the air. My shirt is stuck to my back. Back, arms, legs, head—all aching. The cellar wood is stacked. The heap in the driveway is three-quarters stacked. Floyd could be back in two hours, and there's nothing he'd like better than to catch me with the job not finished.

Opal's been gone all day. Cassie is helping me. Need I say more?

"Why don't you get two Super Sandwiches from the freezer?" I say. "Then you should sit in the shade for a while."

It's a two-over-one row. The bark is dead white and crisp, burns with an oily black smoke, and it'll start a fire if you're ever lost in the woods and you remembered to bring matches.

Cassie comes back with two chocolate sandwiches. Keeping my ears cocked for the Hummer, I sit down in the shade and gulp mine down, then tip back my water bottle and drain it.

Eleven years ago. We're in the backyard. Floyd is throwing the ball and I'm supposed to catch it—we've played this game before. The first couple of times I manage just fine and he smiles at me. It's important to make him smile. I smile back. Then I fumble four catches in a row, the ball rolling away over the grass. When I pick it up for the fourth time and turn around, he's walking up the steps to the side door. His fists are clenched, like he's holding candies he doesn't want me to have. He goes inside. The door shuts. I start to cry.

Man, where did that come from? I drop the empty water bottle on the grass. Ice cream is dripping all over Cassie's fingers as she croons to Rover, something about his nightscares and how she'll look after him.

Standing up, I grip the handles of the wheelbarrow like I'm throttling them. On my way back to the heap of wood, the barrow bangs into the side of the garage because I'm not watching what I'm doing. Terrified, I check the shingles. No damage.

My lucky day.

I fling logs into the wheelbarrow. They *thunk* against the metal, bounce so hard that bark cracks off and chips fly into the air. Sure, Brick, no sign of Lorne or Glenn—go bash some birch logs.

Fire a couple through the living room window straight at Floyd's TV, why don't you?

My throat's so tight I can scarcely breathe, and the wheel-barrow, I see dully, is full.

〜

THE DRIVEWAY'S raked, wheelbarrow leaning against the garage wall with the handles level, new woodpile as geometric as I can make it, and Floyd's home. He jumps to the ground, car-rying his laptop, and strides toward the house. Sometimes (not often), I realize how good-looking he is.

I retreat to the living room, where Cassie's watching *Tree-house*. He comes in holding a sheet of paper and, as usual, ignores Cassie. "Project for you, kiddo," he says. "I had some free time at lunch and found this on the Internet—I want you to take about a third of the wood you've stacked and make a Shaker round. There's a picture here, with a description."

He grins at me, Mr. Charm, *Have I got the lemon for you.* "My father never liked trying anything new. But I'm an innovator. If this works, we'll do all the wood in rounds next summer."

You'd think by now Poker Face would be my middle name.

e grin vanishes. "Is there a problem?"

I shake my head. I'm raining on his parade. Bad idea.

"Sounds neat," I say.

"Drum up a little enthusiasm. Don't they teach you to be open-minded at school?"

"Sure, we'll give it a try."

He tosses the paper on the coffee table. It skids to the floor. "You can start tonight," he says. "Lots of daylight left."

As I bend to pick up the paper, he takes the stairs two at a time. He only does that when he's in a good mood.

A more useful innovation than a round woodpile would be a mood gauge for Floyd, a dial that swings from Terrific through Relatively Neutral to Extraordinarily Bad. Invent one for me. I'll love you forever.

The wood in a Shaker round splays out from the center like the spokes of a wheel. Like the rays on the yellow suns Cassie used to draw.

Last spring the guidance counselor brought in a psychologist to talk about something called "boundaries." *Being able to say* no *is a skill we all need to learn. There are occasions in everyone's life when it's the only appropriate word. Discerning those occasions is also a skill. Saying* no *is one of the most empowering things you can do.* Etc.

She had a decent smile and the girls were lapping it up.

No, Floyd, I won't unstack and restack the woodpile.

Like, hello.

A Shaker round resembles a short fat cylinder with a cone-shaped top. Reminds me of those haystacks that French guy painted, over and over again, in the 1800's. Monet. According to the biography I read, he was "irascible" with his children.

When I go outside and look at the woodpile, so neat and tidy, I realize I'd been thinking that maybe, just maybe, Floyd would say, *Good job, kiddo*. Or even, *Not a bad job, kiddo*.

It's dusk by the time I dismantle a third of the woodpile and rearrange the pallets on the grass. I'll get up early tomorrow, beat the heat.

2.1 [shaker up]

A SHAKER round is a challenge because you have to fill in the spokes as you radiate outward. Also, the outer end of each log will dry quicker than the inner end, so the pile needs to dip toward the center. Sound easy? Try it sometime.

It takes me a while to adjust the diameter, but then I get into the swing of it, and the funny thing is that even though Floyd forced me into making the Shaker round, I forget about him while I'm working on it. In the end the pile looks cool, a hole down the middle for air circulation, logs stacked on top to make a little cone.

It doesn't look like a haystack. More like a mini-fortress in the wilderness. If I had a Canadian flag, I'd stick it in the hole.

If Floyd had a sense of humor.

CASSIE AND I eat supper in the dining room, which is basically a jut off the kitchen. Same tiled floor—faded red and green squares in need of a good polish—along with a dark brown, claw-footed table that weighs a ton, and four chairs. We chow down on Singapore noodles with mixed vegetables, Cassie telling me how Pablo of *The Backyardigans* disguised himself as a ghost and terrified poor Uniqua.

She talks okay, for a little kid. Never said a word until she turned three then came out with whole sentences right away. She keeps this talent under wraps if Floyd's around.

I'm at the kitchen counter loading the dishwasher when the Hummer pulls up. Floyd stays sitting in the cab, hunched over the steering wheel, staring straight ahead. Through the window I can see his fingers drumming on the wheel.

"Cassie," I say, "go upstairs."

I taught her this command after the nightscares began. She picks Rover up by one ear and scrambles up the stairs. The hinges squeal as her bedroom door shuts.

Cassie isn't the problem in this house.

Floyd gets out of the Hummer and locks it. He never slams doors, but tonight it's as though he's being extra careful. I move away from the window, pretty sure he won't bother to check the Shaker round.

His feet scrape on the steps, the mudroom floor creaks, then he opens the kitchen door and steps inside.

I'm five feet ten. He tops me by three inches.

He lays his laptop in its black leather case on the table. "Where's Opal?"

"Out," I say, clearing my throat. "She'll be back later this evening. You had supper?"

He loosens his tie and tosses it on the table. "I lost a sale today," he says. "My client went to Truro, got a better price. You think I should have gone lower?"

Fifty-fifty chance of the wrong answer. "No."

He moves nearer. His eyes are the same color as mine, gray. No light in them.

Worst part is the waiting.

He says, "A family to support—my wife, a useless son, a daughter who behaves as though she's mentally deficient—and you think the forfeiture of a commission is irrelevant?"

"No." I hate it when he piles on the big words.

"No? Is that all you can say?"

Saying no is a skill ... I fight back the sickness rising in my throat. Once, when I was ten, I puked on his new shoes.

I'll say whatever you want me to say. Since I don't know what that is, since nothing I say will be right, I keep my trap shut.

"Pete had the nerve to call me into his office afterward," Floyd says. "He lectured me on how to deal with difficult customers, implied I should have tried harder. One mistake and he treats me as though I'm worthless."

I could say, *That's too bad.* I don't.

Floyd steps closer, so close I can see the stubble on his chin: he's a man who has to shave twice a day. His breath smells of wintergreen.

"After Pete finished his spiel, he pretended to be a boxer, jabbed me a couple of times in the chest. He thought that was funny. Then, do you know what he said?" Floyd doesn't wait for an answer. "That he saw you at the mall bullying a boy much younger than you. Is it true?"

"I only scared him a little. No big deal."

"I'm Pete's head salesman. According to him, your behavior reflects poorly on me, and therefore on GM."

No use to run. Tried that.

I brace myself against the wall.

Slowly Floyd takes off his jacket and arranges it on the back of the nearest chair so the shoulders are level and the sleeves hang free. He rolls up his shirtsleeves. I hope Cassie stays in her room.

There's a pause. A crack in time. His eyes and mine.

A blur of movement, *whump*, and I'm doubled over. Can't breathe, pain roaring through my chest. Then he grabs a handful of my hair, yanks my head up, and starts slapping my face back and forth until I think my neck'll snap like a chicken's.

Tears—I can't stop them—spring to my eyes, spill down my cheeks. He says, slapping as he talks, "I don't need you jeopardizing my relationship with Pete. So this is my other job, to show you who's boss. You're crying like a baby ... How old are you, fourteen going on four?"

His fist sinks into my belly and I go down. I feel like I'm four. Sniveling and pitiful, a coward.

If I wasn't a coward, if I fought back, he'd kill me.

I sneak an upward glance; he's been known to kick me when I'm down. But he's inspecting his knuckles. "I'm going upstairs to have a shower," he says. His shoes have mud on them. They march away.

When I take a breath, the muscles in my side cramp, the pain like a gutting knife between my ribs.

It's over. Until next time.

Which won't be this week or next week. He likes to keep me on edge, though, never knowing when it'll be or what I'll do that will trigger him.

I try to push myself up, then collapse again, sliding down the wall. Too soon. But I don't want Opal to find me here. Or Cassie. Another shallow breath with no cramp this time.

Nothing broken. He's too clever for that. Took boxing when he was a young fellow, prides himself on his control.

My cheeks feel like they're on fire.

Nausea surges up my gullet. I swallow it, sour taste and all. I need to pee. Have to wait until he's out of the bathroom, don't have to be too smart to figure that out. I manage to stand upright, the whole way, leaning against the wall. More sniveling. Pitiful is an understatement.

No black eye. No right to the jaw.

Clutching the back of the couch, I cross the living room. The stairs look as high as Everest. I drag myself up them, step-by-step, terrified of meeting him partway. Lurch over to the wall, edge along it, and then I'm in my room. Very quietly, I close the door.

Floyd has his rules. Never gives me a shiner when school's on. Never uses a belt. Never comes into my room.

Not much of a room, but it's mine. I sit on the bed, hugging my belly, head hanging. And yeah, I'm crying again. Cassie cries less than me, ain't that the truth.

The bathroom door opens, the bedroom door shuts. I wait, willing the pain to subside, knowing it won't until it's good and ready. Something you might be wondering is why don't I juice this up with a few swearwords? He's death on swearing. In grade one I began hanging out with the Donovan boys from Swamp Road; I came home from school one day and reeled off all the neat new words they'd taught me at recess—you know the ones I mean. Floyd belted me clear into the pantry. Hard to say who was more shocked, him or me. Before that, he'd cuffed me on the ear a few times, but nothing major.

That was when the fear started.

By the time I leave my bedroom, the light's out under Cassie's door, Opal's come home, and Floyd's downstairs with her. He won't tell her what happened. He usually lays into me when she's nowhere around, and if he slips up, she turns a blind eye. Probably thinks I deserve it.

I take some Advil and go back to my room. My headphones are broken or I'd listen to some music. A good dose of AC/DC—that's what I need.

You know their song, "Stiff Upper Lip"?

2.2 [heavyweight]

USUAL SETUP the next morning, with Floyd at work and Opal off selling hope and harmony. They're going out for supper, so they won't be back until tonight sometime. Cassie is in the kitchen feeding Cheerios to Rover, scowling at him as she jams the cereal in his face. "You better eat your breakfast," she's saying, "or you'll get a beating." Then she shakes him so hard that Cheerios fly off the table to the floor.

Ever since she started having nightscares, I've done my best to keep her from seeing the crap that goes on in this house. My best obviously isn't good enough.

"Cassie," I say, making her jump, "don't be mean to Rover."

"He's being bad." Another shake, Rover's head flopping up and down.

"Why don't you eat some Cheerios? Show him how."

"Don't want to."

Oh man. "How about I scramble an egg? You like scrambled eggs."

I bend over to find the frying pan, wishing the Advil I just swallowed would kick in. Wishing I didn't feel Cassie tugging at my ankles day and night. "Responsibility" has to be the heaviest word in the dictionary.

I wasn't quite ten when Opal found out she was pregnant. The ruckus she made you'd have thought she had a brain tumor. That's how all three of us discovered her healing powers didn't work when she was the one who needed them.

I sometimes wonder if she kicked up the same fuss before I was born.

Four years ago. Cassie is six weeks old. Opal sashays into the living room one afternoon and dumps baby plus bottle in my lap. "You feed her," she says, "I'm going out."

"No way! She's too young."

Opal's already in the kitchen. As she swings her head around, her earrings bump her neck, silver chains studded with bits of colored glass. "All you have to do is feed her and put her back in the crib."

"But—"

"Stop whining!"

"You can't leave me alone with her."

Her voice sharp enough to cut paper, she says, "I was six weeks old when my mother left me. Dumped me under her sister's lilac bush in an old canvas bag and took off. I don't know—or care—what happened to her, and who knows who my father was. I'm leaving for

*three hours, and you have a mother and a father. You don't know how
lucky you are."*

She's out the side door before I can say another word.

*Cassie's dark blue eyes gaze up at me. I never even held her before.
What if she poops?*

*She smiles at me. Dimples in her fat little cheeks. Her gums two
bumpy pink ridges. Blindly I shove the nipple between them and she
starts to suck. Bubbles gurgle into the bottle. Her eyes stick to mine,
growing heavier and heavier until she falls asleep.*

*I don't know what to do next, so I don't do anything. Just sit
there, feeling the weight of her, somehow knowing this is how it'll be
from now on.*

I got that right.

After beating four eggs into a froth, I pour them in the warm
frying pan and drop bread in the toaster. The eggs cook nice and
fluffy. The toast doesn't burn. But when I reach in the cupboard
for plates, my chest muscles seize up, pain zapping me like an
electric shock.

Cassie says, "He's scary."

Carefully I put the plates on the counter and dole out the
eggs. "Yeah, he is."

"Rover's scared of him too."

Him. He. Like he's God. I sit down across from her and
spoon jam on her toast. "Smart, that skunk. But I'll look after both
of you, Cassie. You don't have to worry about Floyd. Now eat up."

As she digs her fork into the eggs, she's still scowling. On
impulse I say, "Want to go to MacTaggart's Store this morning?"

It's two kilometers away on Route #539, the nearest paved road. "Walk?" she says. She likes dawdling along the road, picking flowers from the ditch. I'm the one who ends up carrying her piggyback.

"We'll take the ATV. As long as we stick to the trails, the cops won't bug us. You have to wear your helmet."

Her scowl's gone like an eraser passed over it. "I saved forty-seven cents."

"You can buy candy."

"Gummi bears."

We follow the trail along the river, then cut in to the store past Beaver Lake. Before Floyd enrolled me in hockey, he taught me to skate there, the winter I was five. I remember asking him, after I'd fallen down for the umpteenth time, why God made ice so hard. I'd heard about God from Kendra, who worked at Happy Whale Daycare; I wasn't sure I wanted two fathers.

"So you'll quit falling down," Floyd said.

But he was patient with me those afternoons at Beaver Lake. He even high-fived me the first time I took off on my own, ankles askew, arms flailing. Mind you, there were often other kids and parents there. Plus he hadn't given up on me yet—he figured I was headed straight for Junior A.

Outside MacTaggart's, I lift Cassie down from the ATV. Once she's standing in front of the glass case, staring at all the different candies, she's not so sure about gummi bears. I wander around the store, wishing I was home in bed.

The third youngest Donovan, a weedy kid called Lucas, is ambling toward the counter, reading the label on a package of caramel chunk cookies. Automatically, I stick my foot out. Down he goes. The package breaks his fall.

"Jeez," I say, "you okay, Lucas?"

He's shaking the package, his face crumpled, and doesn't answer.

Nothing much else in MacTaggart's Store to tempt me. Along with not swearing, I don't smoke or drink. Boring or what.

In her Audrey incarnation, Opal used to smoke. Now that she's into lavender and chamomile, she can smell an unlit cigarette five houses down. Floyd has never smoked. Never touches booze, either. He likes being in control too much—that's my theory.

Maybe it's time to give you the Brick MacAvoy Behavioral Guidelines:

```
(1) Pick on kids smaller than you.
(2) In winter, spread it around: mall, playground,
    school bus. Leave Glenn Semple alone at school
    because he's too popular and you'll get it in
    the neck. The library is off limits.
(3) Always keep a low profile. You never want com-
    plaints to get back to Floyd.
(4) When extorting money, switch from kid to kid and
    keep the amounts small. Also, leave no visible
    bruises, scrapes, or scratches. See (3).


To summarize, be cautious, calculating, and
pragmatic.
```

You may have noticed I hate Floyd using big words even though I do it myself all the time. Chip off the old block. The apple doesn't fall far from the tree.

Okay, so I've wandered off topic.

I reach for the latest ATV magazine, which is when I notice a hand-printed sign pinned to the wall near the magazine rack.

SHINGLES NEED SCRAPING
MUST BE GOOD ON LADDERS
$100
CALL ROLF LANGILLE

Little tabs underneath with a phone number. Rolf Langille lives down the road from us. I tear off the first tab. I like the sound of $100—nice round number. My long-term plan to leave home next year, it'll need money. I'll take the bus from Hilchey Bay to Halifax, where I'll finish high school. Board somewhere, find a part-time job. After that, I'll leave Nova Scotia altogether.

Opal's casual with money; I give her that. As often as I can, I've been stashing a bit away. For instance, after she forked out cash for new Levis and a Reebok T-shirt, I bought them both secondhand at Frenchy's and pocketed the change.

Still, I can almost feel that $100 bill in my pocket, crisp and new. So I treat Cassie to a chocolate bar.

2.3 [♀]

AS WE leave the store, Tully Langille is leaning her bike against the wall. She's Rolf's adopted daughter, fourteen years old, with bright red hair in a thick braid down her back. Anyone else, you might think she dyed it.

She and Glenn started hanging out together as soon as she moved here. Hanging out isn't the same as dating.

We're all in the same grade.

"Hi," she says, looking at Cassie.

Because she's looking at Cassie, I look at her. At the way the wind's flapping her T-shirt against her breasts, to be specific. Our English teacher was hot on specificity.

Breasts? Go ahead, say it. What fourteen-year-old guy calls them breasts?

Melons—too hard.

Knockers, hooters, jugs—no door, no owls, no handles.

Tits—too sharp, like they'd cut you.

Rack—deer antlers? I don't think so.

Boobs—they're no mistake. (Not in my opinion, anyway. In other words, my hormones are in working order, thank you very much.)

Tully's staring at me. Did she just say something? Cassie, as usual, is silent; she's shy with strangers. Tully hunkers down. "I've seen you around, but I've never met you before. Glenn told me your name is Cassie. My name's Tully. What's in the bag?" No response. "Candy, I bet. Can I peek?"

Cassie holds out the bag. "Mmm," Tully says, "an Oh Henry bar. My fave."

Finally Cassie opens her mouth. "Brick buyed it for me."

Tully's eyes flick to mine. "Yeah?" she says.

"He did so!"

"Okay, okay. Can I have a gummi bear?"

Then Tully takes an age deciding which one to take, nattering on about her favorite flavors. I shift my feet. I don't want the whole world seeing me on the front step of MacTaggart's General Store and Gas Bar with my little sister and Tully Langille.

The other girls in our grade have smooth, shiny hair that they toss around a lot. They wear tight jeans with lacy tops designed to spike a guy's testosterone; they talk about guys on the football team and lipstick and something they call *product*.

Not Tully. Baggy clothes, ratty old sneakers, hair like wildfire, and I doubt she knows one end of a lipstick from the other. What drives me nuts is that she doesn't seem to care she's a total loser.

"Rolf home?" I say.

"Why?"

"Gonna ask him about scraping his house."

"You think he'd hire someone like *you*?"

"Why wouldn't he?"

"We both know why not, Brick—I don't want you anywhere near my puppy!"

Cassie says, "Puppy? You gotta puppy? Can I play with it?"

"Your brother doesn't like animals," Tully says. "Any animals."

"He likes Rover," Cassie says.

Tully is one of the few kids in school who isn't scared of me. In February, when she caught me throwing rocks at Igor in his outdoor pen, she screeched loud enough to raise every corpse in the Collings Head Cemetery. Good thing the Semples weren't home—although she threatened to tell them if she saw me anywhere near Igor again.

Then, last spring, even though I'm always super-careful, she glimpsed me picking on Lorne Meisner at school; luckily she wasn't close enough to do anything. If she's told her dad about me, odds are he won't hire me.

I think about the stash of bills under my mattress, scarcely enough for two months' board. "Come on, Cassie," I say, "we'll see if Rolf's home."

Lucas scurries out of the store and picks up his bike. "Ol' MacTaggart gave me a new bag of cookies," he says. "So there, smart ass."

Pumping hard, he takes off. I'll get him for that, even if I have to wait until school starts.

Tully sneers at me. "Bullying the little kids again, Brick?"

"I didn't do anything."

"If you even look at my puppy, I'll—"

"I'm not interested in your dumb puppy! Come *on*, Cassie."

Tully marches into the store, banging the door shut behind her.

Because I'm in a hurry, we drive along the shoulder of #539 to our road, then belt it to Rolf's place. He lives just past Docker Lonergan, who drives the garbage truck one week and the recycling truck the next. Della and Agnes Barnes own the house across the road from us, a bit farther from the river. They have a garden, big time. When she's not primping her roses, Della runs the Hilchey Bay Post Office like she's the CEO of General Motors.

Add the Semples, and that's everyone on Hilchey River Road.

Might as well include the old hunting shack in the woods near the river. Tenants? Porcupines, raccoons, and squirrels.

2.4 [hired hand]

A NOVA Scotia Power truck is parked in Rolf's driveway; he's a lineman. Part of the front of the house has already been scraped.

I park the ATV to the left of the garage under the shade of the trees, where Floyd can't see it from the road, and pocket the key. Floyd's never actually forbidden me to get a job. But he's dead against what he calls *fraternizing with the neighbors*.

After I brush the dust off Cassie's clothes, we walk over to the garage. Rolf comes out. Stocky guy in faded jeans and a black T-shirt.

"Morning," he says.

"I'm good on ladders," I say. "I'll scrape your shingles."

His brow furrows. "You're Floyd's boy?"

"Brick MacAvoy."

"You available the rest of the week and over the weekend?"

"Yeah ... I'm a good scraper, Mr. Langille." *Never done it in my life but how hard can it be?*

"Rolf," he says. "Call me Rolf."

He wouldn't want first names if he knew about Igor and Lorne ... would he?

Tully charges up the driveway on her bike and skids to a halt beside him, huffing and glaring. I wait for her to rat on me, but she doesn't say anything. Then Marigold, her mother, comes out the side door; you can tell right away she's pregnant.

"What's up, Rolf?" she says.

"This here is Floyd's boy. Wants the job."

She has a quiet face, not flashy like Opal's, and curly hair the color of horse chestnuts. She loops her arm through Rolf's, smiling at me. "Are you a good worker, Brick?"

"Sure." My heart sinks. "Only thing is, I got Cassie."

Big-eyed, Cassie is clinging to my leg. But Marigold is like Tully, doesn't give up easy, so we go through another round of gummi bears. By which time I'm sweating bullets—it's as though my entire escape plan depends on this two-bit job.

"I'll like having Cassie here," Marigold says. "She can play with the puppy, and Tully's around."

"Not always," Tully says.

She's still glaring at me. It's not *if* she's planning on ratting, it's *when*.

"Why don't you give Brick a trial run, Rolf?" Marigold says. "See how he does. You start day shifts next Tuesday, Tully can't handle more than the bottom step of any ladder, and I don't want to look at one sideways now I'm pregnant. Besides, no one else has answered your ad." She rests her head on his shoulder. "I bet Brick will do just fine. We need to get started ... it's been too wet all spring to do anything."

I heard Opal tell Floyd that the woman down the road was expecting a baby, a little curl to her lip like, *Why would anyone in her right mind end up pregnant?*

"I can paint too," I say, stretching the truth right out of shape.

Rolf scratches his chin. "Okay," he says, "a trial run. Start around this side of the house—Tully can scrape the lower part later. Thorough, that's what I want. No skimping. But no digging into the shingles, either. I like wooden shingles better than siding, so I don't want them ruined."

"Is the ATV all right under the trees? I try not to park in the sun because I don't want the paint to fade."

"No problem."

I bend down and whisper fiercely, "Cassie, you be a good girl and stay out of everybody's way."

"Puppy," she whispers back.

"Be gentle with the puppy."

Tully gives a rude snort. Perfect opening for her to say something about Igor.

Not a word.

I didn't know she was scared of heights, a fact I stow away for future reference. As Marigold and Cassie go indoors, Rolf passes me a paint scraper and two sheets of sandpaper. The ladder's leaning against the wall. I start to climb it, feeling it shift under my weight. I hope I'm not scared of heights.

I wish Tully wasn't watching.

Old paint's flaking off the shingles. I start at the top row, counting out twelve shingles, which is as far as I can reach without my ribs screeching in protest. Even though the shingles are smooth, not ridged, the scraper has a mind of its own.

"Not so hard," Rolf says, "or you'll cut into the wood."

You're clueless, kiddo.

A flake comes off, neat as can be. "That's better," he says, and watches for a few more minutes. "Don't forget to sand the edges ... there's lots more sandpaper. You need anything, just holler. Otherwise I'll leave you to it."

He and Tully head for the front of the house. Through the open window, I can hear Cassie's and Marigold's voices. The sun is hot on my back, the wind sighing through the treetops, and right now, all I'm responsible for is a scraper and a few shingles.

AN HOUR later Rolf comes back, stationing himself by the ladder and looking over the part I've finished. He's going bald on top.

"Your edges are smooth," he says, nodding in approval, "and you're down to bare wood where the paint's flaked, that's good." Real warmth in his voice.

Don't tell me I'm doing something right for a change.

He hands me a few fresh sheets of sandpaper and a bottle of water, gives the shingles another once-over, then disappears again. I take a swig from the bottle, shove it in my back pocket, and keep going, switching to my left hand because my right arm's aching, tugging my ball cap around so the brim protects my neck from the sun. Another hour passes. I concentrate on the rows I've done, not on how many are left.

I'm into the rhythm of it now, no thought required, just the rasp of the scraper and the rustle of wind through the leaves. At midday, Marigold calls through the window, "Sandwiches made, Brick. Come on in."

I finish the last two shingles in the row and climb awkwardly down the ladder. My legs feel numb, my shoulders are sore, and I can feel each imprint of Floyd's fists; but one whole section's scraped top to bottom. I hope I did an okay job.

I've never eaten a meal in anyone else's house. I kick off my sneakers at the side door, which leads right into the kitchen. First thing you know, a fluffy brown puppy is sniffing my socks.

Cassie says, "His name's Caramel. Can we have a puppy?"

"Nope."

"Pat him, Brick. He likes having his ears scratched."

The whole crew's lined up—Rolf and Marigold smiling, Tully thin-lipped. The puppy butts me with his head. I stoop, trying not to wince, and rub him between the ears. He closes his eyes, leans into me.

Big folds of skin around his neck, waiting for him to grow into them.

Funny thing, I've thrown more than my share of rocks at dogs, but I've never actually touched one before. Not even—but this isn't the time for that particular memory. Cassie plops down beside me and shoves her face into the puppy's fur. He slurps at her chin with his tongue. She giggles.

Marigold says, "The bathroom's down the hall, Brick. There's a clean towel on the counter."

So far, so good. Tully hasn't blabbed about Igor, Lorne, or Lucas. Or the other Donovan kids or Gary Sanger or Billy Gottrich. I wash up in the bathroom, which is old-fashioned, superclean, and has blue towels that match the picture on the wall of a sailboat on the ocean. It's only a photo out of a calendar, but the frame's handmade.

The kitchen window overlooks the trees out back. I sit down at the table and, when the plate's passed, help myself to a sandwich and a chunk of cheese. Cassie, who hardly ever talks to Opal and never to Floyd, is burbling away to anyone who'll listen. I try to relax. The sandwiches are ham and lettuce.

Rolf says, "The job's yours if you want it, Brick. But you gotta put in long hours while the weather holds, so I need to know I can depend on you."

"You can," I say. Praying she's behaved herself, I add, "Is Cassie a bother?"

"She's no trouble," Marigold says.

Marigold and Rolf moved to Hilchey Bay late last December, right after they got married. Like I said, even though Tully has Rolf's last name, she isn't Rolf's kid. If anyone at school asks about her real father, she clams up. If they persist, she turns nasty. Tully can do nasty in spades.

Marigold puts a plate of cookies on the table. I take one. Peanut butter, melt in your mouth. "Some good," I say and take another.

"I made them," Tully says.

I look down at my plate, wishing this meal was over. At home, Cassie and I eat on our own.

After lunch, I move the ladder over the window and scrape

the shingles above it, wearing gloves that Rolf gave me against blisters. I like how he's leaving me alone to do the job, whistling away to himself as he scrapes the front. More of a meander than a tune. Still, it's a happy sound.

Floyd watches every move and lists every single thing you're doing wrong until—of course—you start making real mistakes.

What if Floyd finds out about this job?

Marigold cooks supper for us, fried chicken and potato salad with homemade tea biscuits. Then I scrape like a maniac on the far side of the house, the one you can't see from the road. That $100 is as good as mine.

I don't imagine you're dying of suspense to know how meals work at our place—but be patient. There is a point.

Every two months Opal loads up the freezer. When she's home, she eats salads from Sobeys, and she and Floyd often eat out; I don't have to cook for them, which, believe me, is a major perk. Cassie and I start at the top of the freezer and work our way to the bottom. Also, Opal puts money in a jar in the pantry for extra groceries like eggs, bananas, and peanut butter, for my school lunches, and for clothes for me and Cassie. She doesn't count the change. That's how I've accumulated most of my stash. I told you there was a point.

The stash is money I've stolen. Opal refuses to pay me for babysitting. Who says two wrongs can't make a right?

It's nearly nine o'clock before I clamber down the ladder and lean against the wall. *Exhausted* has a whole new meaning. Wriggling my shoulders, feeling my right arm hang heavy, I take a few deep breaths. My ribs still hurt, but not half as bad as my hands. Gloves or no gloves, both thumbs are blistered.

Making me jump, Rolf says, "You done good, Brick. Get here as early tomorrow as you can. Want me to pay you as you go, or wait until we're done?"

"Wait," I say, hoping he didn't notice me leap in the air like a startled rabbit.

Cassie's nearly asleep when I load her against my chest on the ATV. Just to be safe, we connect behind Rolf's with the river trail and follow it home, headlights picking out the boulders, boughs brushing the handlebars.

The house crouches in the trees, its windows small and so close together it looks cross-eyed. It was built in 1899 by my great-great-grandfather, a sea captain who didn't want to look at the ocean on his days off. According to local legend, his crew members never signed up for a second stint.

Both vehicles are parked by the garage. I shouldn't have stayed so long at Rolf's—what's wrong with me? My brain scurries for a cover story. Late supper and a visit to the toy department at Zellers is the best I can come up with.

Carrying Cassie inside nearly finishes me off. As I enter the kitchen, I stop in my tracks. Floyd's playing his guitar in the living room. Johnny Cash, "Just the Other Side of Nowhere." Remember the mood gauge? Johnny Cash means Floyd's hovering at the high end of Terrific.

One Christmas I found a T-shirt with Johnny Cash's picture on it, and gave it to him—he wore it Christmas Day, Boxing Day, and New Year's Eve. He still sometimes wears it on weekends.

"Thanks, Son." That's what he said. *Thanks, Son.*

He's tucked in the far corner of the living room, fingers plucking the strings, face relaxed. My breath escapes in a long sigh. Cassie doesn't seem as heavy as she was a few minutes ago.

Once she's in bed, I turn AC/DC on low and read about yaks and yurts.

3.1 [wheels and deals]

I'M UP early the next morning. Floyd's downstairs, so I give
the bathroom a swipe—one of my regular chores. Every morning
he leaves wet towels on the floor, shaving cream gobbed on the
sink, toothpaste stuck to the counter, yesterday's boxers tossed in
the direction of the hamper but not quite making it. At least he
flushes.

We pass on the stairs. I can't read his mood; I'll wait until he's
gone before I wake Cassie.

Because Marigold will feed us our meals, I make do with cereal for breakfast. I'm crunching away, reading the Arctic book,
when Floyd positions himself in the doorway. "I just checked the
bathroom. You didn't wipe the mirror and you left a couple of
hairs in the tub."

His hairs.

"Cleaning a bathroom isn't neurosurgery, kiddo."

"Soon as I finish eating, I'll fix it."

"How about you fix it right now."

So I hoof it upstairs, spray the mirror with Windex and the tub with Fantastik, and the whole time he's watching me.

"You might as well clean the toilet while you're here," he says, inspecting his fingernails.

Just once, I wish I had the guts to argue.

By the time I sit down at the kitchen table again, the cereal's gone to mush. To top it off, Floyd is in no hurry to leave because he has a Chamber of Commerce meeting this evening and he's gathering his notes.

It's 9:10 before the Hummer backs out of the driveway. I wake Cassie and hustle her into her clothes. She fusses, whining for the blue T-shirt, not the pink one.

"Okay, okay," I say, "just hurry up!"

I make toast, grab a couple of bananas, and load Cassie, Rover, and a bunch of her toys onto the ATV. At Rolf's I park under the trees again. Munching on her toast, Cassie goes indoors.

The ladder's leaning against the wall. While I'm coating my arms with sunscreen, Rolf comes out of the garage. "Hey there," he says cheerfully. "Another sunny day." He passes me the scraper. "I sharpened the blade some. Once you finish this wall, you can start the back—it'll be in the shade."

Tully stays out of my face all day, and Marigold helps me bundle Cassie onto the ATV that evening. "She took a nap," she says. "She's a cutie. See you tomorrow."

"Okay," I say. She's still standing there, a quizzical look on her face as though she's waiting for something. "Um, thanks for everything."

She smiles. "You're welcome."

She really means it. How nice is that.

The scraping's nearly finished, Tully's kept her mouth shut, and I'm feeling cocky. I'll go home along the road.

I back around the garage, then brake at the end of Rolf's driveway to check for logging trucks. Two ATVs are charging toward us in a billow of dust, the nearer one Snyder McIsaac's. Snyder is in grade eleven and totals the most penalties for fighting of any player in Midget B.

I move up to Midget in the fall. Weird to think we'll be on the same team. Or do I mean downright terrifying?

The ATVs stop in front of me, engines snarling.

Snyder says, "If it ain't Brick MacAvoy, only player in the league who's never scored a goal. Should've known you'd be a nanny in your spare time."

The other guy thrusts his face at Cassie, his teeth bared in a ferocious grin. She cowers against me.

I can't take to the ditch because it's full of rocks. Snyder clambers off his machine and stands next to me so that I have to look up at him. Looking up at someone enforces submission. I read that somewhere.

Then Rolf strolls up and parks himself beside my ATV, hands on his hips. Pitching his voice over the engine noise, he says, "Why don't you guys move along?"

I can see Snyder weighing the odds. He laughs, thumbs

hooked in his jeans like Floyd—except Snyder isn't lean and mean, he's chubby and mean. "Guess we're blocking your driveway."

"You're scaring the little girl," Rolf says. "We don't like thugs on this road."

"No need to be insulting," Snyder says.

He saunters back to his ATV and in an aggressive roar sets off toward #539, his buddy trailing, smothered in dust. Rolf says, "You're in a tough crowd if you hang with them, Brick."

"They're not friends of mine."

Rolf's eyes sharpen. "You doing drugs?"

"No! Never have."

"I've heard Snyder and his crew are dealers—and can turn real nasty real quick." He looks right at me. "One thing I can't abide is strong-arm stuff."

He strides back to the house.

I drive Cassie home. Snyder won't forget that little incident in a hurry. He'll be in grade twelve the year I'm new kid on the block at the regional high school. Now that *is* downright terrifying. It's also one more reason to leave Hilchey Bay the day I turn sixteen.

After I put Cassie to bed, I read to her from *Horton Hears a Who!* Cassie really likes the idea that you're somebody even though you're small.

Her eyelids are drooping. I close her door and have a long, hot shower. Five or six years ago, Opal ordered Floyd to renovate her office, their bedroom, and the bathroom; the rest of the house could fall down around her ears for all she'd care. Seashells decorate the ceramic tile, with a shower curtain to match. Pearl-gray bathmat and towels, brushed pewter taps. Opal's soaps and lotions smell like Della Barnes's flower garden.

Opal's no rosebud. She doesn't need anyone lecturing her about boundaries. Opal's a border crossing, armed guards everywhere, and me with no passport.

Even after all that hot water pummeling my muscles, they're still complaining. Seems as good a time as any to start one of the books I took out of the library, the autobiography of the tennis player, Andre Agassi. Then, of course, I'm hooked. When he was only seven years old, his father forced him to hit balls for hours every day. As a kid, he was scared of his father. As a champion, he hated tennis.

I'm scared of Floyd and I hate hockey. Logically, I should be on the fast track to the NHL.

3.2 [don't cry over spilled ...]

LIGHTS OFF around midnight, so I wake up later in the morning than I planned. Bathroom's empty, but from the hall I can hear Opal and Floyd talking downstairs, Floyd's voice tight.

"I told you, sales were down last month and they're not happy at head office. Pete did his Big Boss act yesterday, with the result that I've been moved to this morning's schedule ... do you think I'd be going to work on a Saturday otherwise? He's even thinking of putting me on Saturdays permanently ... There's a sale I've almost nailed down. He'd better not run interference."

I tiptoe to the bathroom, praying he'll leave in the next few minutes. But when I cross the living room, he's still at the dining-room table, coffee in his Eric Lindros mug, nose buried in the classified section of the paper. Cassie's cereal bowl has a small pool of milk in it, sprinkled with a few Cheerios. She's blowing on them; they're floating, like those rings you toss to people who are drowning.

She reaches for the milk carton, not watching what she's doing. Over it goes. Milk streams across the plastic tablecloth toward Floyd's newspaper.

Frozen to the floor, I let out a croak of dismay. The milk soaks into the bottom of the paper. Floyd lowers the paper, sees the milk carton, then sees me. He surges to his feet. "Look what she's done!"

Cassie jams herself against the rungs of her chair, white-faced.

From the pantry, Opal calls, "Want more coffee, Floyd?"

"No thanks," he says, "I'd better be off."

He pushes his chair away from the table. "She's ruined my paper, kiddo. It's your job to look after her, stop her from being so clumsy."

She's four years old. You scared her.

He takes a step toward me. "Wipe that look off your face."

"Sorry, sorry ... I'll clean up the mess."

I'm sorry, I'm sorry. Years ago I used to say that to Floyd, thinking it would help.

"Get yourself out of bed in the mornings," he says, "show some initiative."

I drop my eyes. The One and Only Chinless MacAvoy, Live at a Theater Near You. *Chinless Wonder* is one of Floyd's favorite taunts. Wimp, loser, dummy, gutless, useless, clueless—I've heard 'em all.

"By the way," he says, "the bathroom floor needs wiping."

He heads for the pantry. He always kisses Opal good-bye

whether he's leaving for five minutes or five days.

Every nerve in my body is screaming at me to hightail back upstairs and wipe the floor. The fear on Cassie's face is what stops me. That, and knowing it's my fault. She isn't normally clumsy. She spilled the milk because she's tired, and the reason she's tired is because I've had her out late two days in a row.

"I'll clean up the mess, Cassie," I say, patting her shoulder. "He'll be gone to work soon."

I mop up the milk and rinse the cloth, leaving the tap running so I won't hear the sounds of the clinch in the pantry. Sex is how Opal keeps Floyd in line, that's another of my theories. Although, believe me, I don't spend much time thinking about it.

One more theory and then I'll quit—he'd never dare hit Opal. They come out of the pantry, his hand on her hip, her arm around his waist. I drape the cloth over the edge of the sink. Then he's out the door. Opal says, smug as a cat, "I'm going back to bed."

"We'll be gone all day," I say. She doesn't bother asking where we'll be.

I'll have to take the ATV to Rolf's again to keep up the pretence that we're at the beach, the library, or the mall. Still, I got off easy this morning; Floyd could have socked me, to keep me in line. Or, to use his phrase, as *punishment for an infraction*.

As Opal climbs the stairs, I lay the paper flat to dry. Once their bedroom door shuts, I say, the words like stones in my throat, "Cassie, you haven't told Rolf or Marigold about Floyd, have you? About the bad stuff he does?"

"Nope."

"I should've warned you. You mustn't tell them, or Tully. Promise?"

She nods, twiddling Rover's ear.

"From now on," I add, "you'd better wait and have breakfast with me."

She nods again. She's wearing the same clothes as yesterday, none too clean, but I'm not about to have her change them. "I'll make toast and we'll go to Marigold's place."

So that's what we do.

3.3 [three's a crowd]

MARIGOLD'S OUT on the step, sitting in the sun with her coffee, the puppy curled at her feet. "Hi, Brick, hi, Cassie. I made blueberry pancakes, want some?"

Cassie's eyes light up. "Yep."

My mouth's watering. "Nah, gotta finish the scraping."

Last night I left the ladder out back. When I go around the corner, Tully and Glenn are standing there, each gripping one end of it. I hold tight to my temper. Can't touch smart-ass Glenn Semple here.

Tully says, "I've been watching you. Acting so nice to your little sister. Stroking Caramel. Why did you throw rocks at Igor that day?"

"Gimme the ladder—I've got work to do."

"We're not letting go until you tell us."

*Three months ago. Floyd trashing me all the way back from the rink
because I got a penalty for high-sticking. I throw on a jacket and stomp
down the road. No sign of Glenn, but here's this stupid greyhound
looking happy as can be in his fenced enclosure. Green vinyl chain-link
fence with tall metal posts.*

*The fence is what pushed me over the edge. Dog didn't even have
the smarts to jump over it.*

Always plenty of rocks on Hilchey River Road.

The same rage is vibrating along my limbs right now. "I only hit
him twice. What's all the fuss about?"

"You scared him," Glenn says hotly.

The sun catches in Tully's hair like firecrackers. Her eyes narrow. "Seems as though you don't bully Cassie. I know you don't
bully me. But you bully Lucas and Lorne, and Gary Sanger."

Bully? Excuse me. All I do is hassle kids to have a bit of fun,
or to blow off steam. And why didn't she add Glenn to the list?

Duh. Because he hasn't told her.

"I never pick on girls," I say. "I have my standards."

Glenn says, "I overheard your father reaming out the receptionist when my dad was pricing a new car. Humiliating her in
front of—"

"Shut up!" I shove him hard in the chest.

He staggers and bangs into the wall, dropping the ladder.
"Do that again," he says, "I dare you!"

Taking a fistful of his T-shirt, I haul him toward me. Tully
drops her end of the ladder and tugs at my elbow. He kicks me
in the shin. When I kick him back, her ankle gets in the way.

"Ouch!" she cries.

"Tully," Rolf calls, "you seen the other scraper?"

My breath escapes in a *whoosh*. I unclench my fist, leaving a little bundle of creases in Glenn's shirt. I'd have smucked him without a thought for the consequences. No job. No $100.

You'd have lost more than that.

My shin hurts where Glenn's sneaker hit bone.

Rolf comes around the corner. "Problem here?"

"No," says Glenn.

I wait for Tully to tell on me.

She's frowning at Glenn. Guess she was waiting for him to do the same thing. "No," she says. As she steps back, bumping into the ladder, it scrapes against a rock.

"Easy," Rolf says, "ladders don't grow on trees."

"Specially metal ones," Tully says, flashing him a smile. He smiles back and ruffles her hair. "I left the scraper beside the paint can," she says, "I'll show you." As she leads him off to the garage, I try to imagine Rolf's smile on Floyd's face.

I don't understand why Tully is keeping her mouth shut. What's in it for her? She never struck me as the devious type.

Glenn smoothes the creases in his T-shirt. I could clock him right now and who'd know? But my limbs feel like lead and I've got no heart for it.

"What are you here for?" I say.

"Tully asked if I'd help Rolf with the painting. It's supposed to rain in a couple of days, and he wants to get the whole house finished beforehand."

"Why do you hang out with Tully? She's such a loser."

"I like her! We're friends."

"You must be her only friend in Hilchey Bay."

"That makes the rest of you losers," Glenn says, flicking out a fist.

Floyd could teach him a thing or two about punching. "Why aren't you scared of me?"

He blinks. "I am scared."

"Then why don't you holler when I twist your arm? And why haven't you told Tully?"

"Not my style."

What's style got to do with it? I fling the ladder up against the house and go at the last of the shingles as if my life depends on it. Doesn't he understand that's why I have to keep at him—because he won't give in?

Because he never cries.

WHEN I head indoors to take a leak, Glenn's balanced on a stepladder, painting the top shingles on the front of the house. Tully's painting the bottom ones. The paint is a cheerful shade of yellow. Sitting in the grass, weaving a crown of dandelions for Rover, Cassie is singing to herself how she's a small person who's somebody ...

Glenn. Igor. Tully. Cassie. Floyd. It's a wonder I can climb the back step, I feel so heavy.

Cassie never sings at home.

I gotta stick closer to her. Shield her from seeing Floyd beat on me.

*Six months ago. I've just finished shoveling the snow away from the
garage doors, while Cassie's been building a Rover-sized snow fort.
We're both hungry. Indoors, as I beat eggs with the electric hand mixer,
she looks for canned mushrooms in the pantry.*

*Floyd marches into the kitchen. "I told you not to put salt on the
steps!"*

"But the ice—"

*His ring catches me on the ear. The beaters spray eggs over the
canisters and the counter. Then it's a fist to the gut.*

Cassie is trapped in the pantry, watching me get sucker-punched.

Although it wasn't much of a set-to by Floyd's standards, it was
enough to start her nightscares. A couple of days later, I taught
her the go-upstairs command.

I have to protect her. Try and make up for Floyd's meanness
and Opal's indifference. What else did Horton say? Something
about not letting his small persons drown …?

How I'm going to manage all this I don't know.

I hardly say a word at lunch, pea soup with grilled cheese
sandwiches. Cassie chatters away like a normal kid would, I guess.
Rolf says he plans on working tomorrow, Sunday, even though
his old dad will be banging on the lid of his coffin.

Marigold brings out a plate of chocolate chip cookies and puts
them right in front of me. At Happy Whale, when I was little,
Kendra used to bake cookies that were loaded with chocolate, moist
and chewy. Memories of Kendra … one more layer of heaviness.

"No thanks," I say, and push back from the table.

ROLF HAS me priming a few bare spots next. Then he hands me a new brush and a gallon can of yellow paint. "I already stirred it," he says. "Don't apply it so thick it drips, or so thin you can see the old color underneath. Work the paint into the brush as you go. Where d'you want to start?"

"This side of the house is fine," I say. It can be seen from the road, but Floyd's shift won't end before four.

I'm terrified of spilling the paint—*you're such a loser, kiddo*—so it takes me forever to climb the ladder and settle the can on the shelf at the top. I slosh the brush in the paint, scrape it on the edge of the can, and make the first swipe. Paint drips from the bottom edge of the shingles. I try again, forcing myself to calm down.

Eventually I get the knack of how much paint to leave on the brush. Painting feels like a vacation after scraping, and as Outdoor Latex Sunshine Yellow takes over from blah beige, I settle in. Even edging the windows and the door isn't a problem. First thing you know, I've done all the top shingles and go looking for Rolf.

"Tully can do the rest," he says, surveying the wall and nodding in approval. As Marigold joins us, he says, "Looks some nice, don't it?"

She gives a sigh of pure pleasure. "I love the color, Rolf. It's perfect. If we can get the first coat on today, second coat tomorrow, then it can rain from dawn till dusk. We can easily finish the shutters in the garage, and the window trim won't take long."

"We still gotta paint the window boxes."

"Wedgwood blue, like the shutters," she says dreamily. "I'll plant them full of petunias."

As he puts his arm around her shoulders, they smile at each other like they're the best of friends.

Rolf says, "Okay, Brick—Glenn's working on the other side of the house. Why don't you start at the opposite end of the wall from him, so the two of you meet in the middle? Then Marigold and Tully can paint the lower part. I'll tackle the doors."

He talks to me like we're equals. I'd better not get used to it. Or to meals that are put in front of me. I move my stepladder around the house and start painting. At the far corner Glenn has his iPod strapped to his arm, the earpieces in, his brush moving to the music.

Why would I want a fricking iPod?

I start painting. We move our stepladders closer. As he swings his around, it whacks me on the leg. I bang mine against the wall and rush him.

He lifts the ladder like a shield, and he's laughing at me. Laughing. At me. "Rolf's just round the corner," he says, and now he's thrusting with the ladder as if it's a spear. "And Marigold thinks you're such a nice guy—you wouldn't want to blow it."

Then he sticks his earpiece back in, picks up his paint can, and climbs the ladder. He's going to reach the top of the window before me. He had a head start. I'm up my ladder with my brush in the can before you can say *paint*.

Cassie comes around the corner, dragging Rover. "I want to go home."

"You can't."

"I want my Princess Melanie baking set."

"We'll bring it tomorrow."

"I want it now!"

I miss a strip, go back, paint over it. She can keep this up for hours.

She says, "I'll go get it."

"You're not allowed on the road by yourself."

She drops Rover on the grass and kicks him. "You're a big meanie, Brick."

I hope Glenn has the volume on high. I move the stepladder nearer the window. Ten minutes and I'll be done. "Where's Tully?"

"Painting. I want someone to play with."

There's days I wish you'd never been born. Let's face it, there's entire years I wish you'd never been born.

"Where's Caramel?"

"In his crate. I am so going to fetch my baking set all by myself."

"No, you're not!"

She plops down on the grass, drums her heels, and screams. Volume high. No tears.

Glenn pulls out his earpiece. "What's up, Cassie? Mad at your brother? But he's such a nice guy."

Marigold comes on the run. "Is everyone too busy to pay attention to you, Cassie? How about I set up the sprinkler and you can run through it?"

The scream stops in midair; the two of them walk away hand in hand. Waiting until they're out of sight, Glenn says, "Are you planning on throwing rocks at Igor again?"

"Depends."

"If you do, I'll borrow Dad's digital camera and catch you in action. You wouldn't want me to mail a print to your father."

Drips slop from my brush. "Not your style," I say.

"You passing your garbage along only makes it smell worse."

"Yes, Reverend."

"Are you gonna throw rocks at Caramel?"

"Are you gonna drop dead?"

He's laughing again. "Wouldn't that be convenient."

I picture the paint can upended on his head, Sunshine Yellow slithering down his face. "You won't always be at Rolf's."

"Stating the obvious is the sign of a lazy mind." His brush comes almost to the edge of where I've painted. "I'll finish up here," he adds. "You can start the back."

"I don't take orders from—"

"Lunchtime!" Marigold calls from the back step.

"Don't eat all the sandwiches," Glenn says and shoves his earpiece back in.

You wait until the next time I catch you on the bridge with your stupid dog.

I END up alongside Rolf for the back wall; he paints and whistles. I paint. Next, in the garage, we coat the window boxes with wood sealant. The two of us, working together.

As we rinse the brushes in the sink in the garage, Rolf says, "You're a good worker, Brick. You want a reference anytime, you just ask."

"Oh. Er, thanks."

"We should finish the second coat in plenty of time tomorrow.

Tuesday's pay day. I'll get cash at the bank machine and you can pick it up here at the end of my shift."

"I'm cool with that."

I'll open an account at the bank on Wednesday and put my whole stash in it. A year from December and I'm outta here.

Seventeen months from now. A room of my own in Halifax. I don't care if it's only eight-by-ten, providing it's mine. With a key so I can lock the door. Enough money for meals would be a bonus. The room won't be big enough for hockey gear. Isn't that too bad?

It's around eight by the time I load Cassie on the ATV. "Say good night."

Natural as can be, Cassie lifts her face to Marigold, who hugs her and drops a kiss on her cheek. I can't remember the last time Opal kissed Cassie.

I should never have taken this job.

We drive home along the road. As we pull up by the garage, Floyd's holding the car door open for Opal, him wearing slacks and a blazer, her in a long red dress. I turn off the ignition and stay put, deeply thankful we left Rolf's before Floyd drove past.

"You're spending a lot of time away from home, kiddo. New girlfriend?"

He knows I've never had a girlfriend.

"Good thing Cassie's along as a chaperone," he adds, jovial for him. "If you need us, we're at The Black Schooner—the restaurant in Collings Harbor."

The house would have to be burning down before I'd need you, Floyd.

Once the taillights disappear around the bend, I do a little shuffle in the driveway. After Cassie's in bed, I can make garlic-flavored popcorn and watch TV. Or google stuff on Floyd's laptop.

Cassie wants me to read *Oh, the Places You'll Go!* She's asleep by page four. Downstairs, the movie channel wins over the laptop. I line up two cans of Coke and the popcorn and settle in.

3.4 ["If You Want Blood (You've Got It)" or "Night of the Long Knives," take your pick]

THE PAINTING'S done by mid-afternoon the next day. Glenn, Tully, Rolf, Marigold, Cassie, and me, we all traipse around the house admiring it, me feeling kind of stupid. Just the same, I'll miss coming here. Despite Tully and Glenn, it's been a like a vacation.

Although how would I know? MacAvoy vacations are Adults Only.

"First fine day I'll hang the shutters," Rolf says.

"I'll go to the nursery and pick out some annuals," Marigold says. "You and Cassie must come for supper one day next week, Brick, when everything's finished."

"Chicken fingers," Cassie says.

Back at the house, the Malibu isn't in the driveway. Sunday

afternoons, Floyd and Opal either head for Dartmouth Crossing, the big shopping area west of here, or up to New Glasgow. Opal is a big fan of Sunday shopping. They usually eat out on the way home.

We have the place to ourselves for at least two hours.

Cassie knows the routine. "I want to watch *Nemo*," she says.

"Again?"

"Yep. First, will you read that book about all the places we'll go?"

I roll my eyes. But she's grinning at me, just like she grinned at Marigold and Rolf the last few days, and I want to keep that happiness right where it is. So we sit on the couch and read *Oh, the Places You'll Go!* To my dismay, it goes to some dark places ... bang-ups and lurches and scary things that watch you with mean little eyes. But Cassie doesn't seem to mind, because by the end of the story, we're guaranteed pretty much a ninety-nine percent chance of success.

"I got brains and shoes with feet inside," Cassie says.

"You sure do. How about I make you popcorn?"

"The pink sugary kind."

Once she's all set, I go into Floyd's study, which is just off the living room, and turn on his laptop. I spend some time googling Arctic islands, which leads me to Greenland and Inuit hunters. Then I insert the library DVD of the concert AC/DC gave years ago in Madrid; Floyd has speakers for the laptop so he can listen to Johnny Cash.

The concert is in Plaza de Toro, a huge amphitheater where spotlights roam the crowd. All those upturned faces, screaming

and whistling, more people than I've seen in my entire life. Angus
is in high gear. In his shorts and striped tie, he races around the
stage, bare knees pumping, curly hair flopping, hitting on his guitar like it's alive.

"Cassie," I call, "come and watch this."

She brings the metal bowl of popcorn with her, carefully putting it down on the floor before she climbs up into my lap.
"Noisy," she says.

"You bet. Watch the guy with the shorts."

She bounces to the rhythm. Then she slides down and starts
to dance, waving her arms as wildly as the people in the crowd,
stamping her shoes with her feet inside, and the whole time she's
giggling. We've brought our Rolf-and-Marigold selves home with
us, I suddenly realize. Rolf, who praised my work; Marigold, who
always made sure there was a clean towel for me on the bathroom
counter, and who kissed Cassie good night. We were ourselves
there. Normal. Carefree.

I crank the volume up several notches and begin clapping to
the beat, laughing at Cassie who's laughing at me.

"What's going on here?"

Cassie freezes, her arms over her head. My palms connect—
clap!—before I can stop them. AC/DC keeps bellowing out the
lyrics and the fans scream their heads off.

Automatically I move the cursor to the exit button. Silence
rings in my ears.

Floyd marches across the room, brushing past Cassie and
nearly knocking her off her feet. Her arms jerk down like she's a
puppet.

I stand up. He cracks me across the face, flinging me sideways.

All I can see is Cassie's face, frozen in terror. Not a trace of laughter left.

Anger explodes like a grenade in my chest. I rush him, plant my hand on his shirt and shove him backward. "Can't you even wait until she's out of the room? Cassie, go upstairs—right now!"

She starts for the door, trips over the bowl of popcorn, and falls down. Her elbow thuds against the leg of the desk. "Run, Cassie!"

Then I'm on to him, jabbing my fists anywhere I can find an opening. "I hate your guts—I hate your goddamn guts!"

Cassie scurries through the door.

Floyd's fist connects with my ear. But I don't go down. No sir. I'm flailing at him—fists, toes, knees, elbows—and they're connecting too. "What do you care about her? You only care about yourself, you sonofabitch."

His face, astounded, when I punch him in the ribs.

I kick his ankle. The bowl of popcorn goes flying, clanging across the floor. I punch out again, wanting to scare the crap out of him the same way he scares Cassie, my heart pounding in triumph when I land another one straight to his gut. His muscles softer than I expected. My knuckles sink in.

He snarls like a wild animal, his face convulsed. Then he comes at me, faster than I can see, too fast for me to duck. Fists to my jaw, my cheek, my eye. I'm backing up, panicked, then I hit the wall, a picture frame cutting into my shoulder. His Salesman of the Year award.

He ploughs me in the chest. I jacknife. He hauls me up by the hair, hits me in the belly, and lands a vicious kick on my shin. I don't even know if I'm crying because inside I'm howling, begging him to stop—but I can't get a word out, he's going to kill me and there's nothing I can do to stop him.

"*Floyd!*"

The fists stop. I drop to my knees, huddled over, chin to my chest. Then I tumble sideways, curled like a fetus on the floor. Clawing, brutal pain ... no room left for me.

He's finally gotten rid of me.

Words float overhead. "He attacked me. *Attacked* me."

A rustle of fabric and two small thumps, like knees against the floor. Perfume drifts to my nose. Then a hand rests briefly on my shoulder. "Brick," Opal says, "are you all right? Can you hear me?"

She touched me. Opal touched me.

A strangled sound comes out of my throat.

The floorboards creak as she stands up. "Floyd, I don't care what Brick did. You've gone too far."

"If I choose to discipline my son, that's my business."

"If you kill your son, that's everyone's business!"

"Lay off, Opal!"

"What if you've broken his ribs? How are you planning to explain that?"

Sullen. "I'm no fool—I didn't hit hard enough to break anything."

"I hope you're right—for your sake and his." Steel in her voice. "You're not Thaddeus. You should quit behaving like him."

"Keep your cheap psychology. It's fake. Your whole gig's fake."

"And yours isn't? Let me sell you this brand-new four-by-four—you'll be a big success, you'll be happy, the women will think you're a stud."

"If I didn't sell cars, you couldn't drive the roads day and night."

"If we lived in town, I wouldn't need a car."

I try to move. Too much trouble.

Try to open my eyes. Right eye stays shut. Left eye, floor level, gives me a close-up of pink popcorn, crusted with sugar. My stomach heaves. A drill's gnawing its way through my jaw.

Opal sighs. "Why did Brick attack you?"

"Ask him."

"Whose popcorn is that on the floor?"

"Can't a man get any peace inside his own house?"

She says, voice back to steel, "We're going to help him up to bed. You'd better pray he doesn't need a doctor."

My left eye is suddenly filled with the flowers on her skirt. She says, "Brick, you have to stand up. We'll both help as much as we can. Floyd, take his other arm ... gently!"

The next five minutes are best forgotten. Floyd doesn't know *gentle*, and although Opal tries to shield me, she's not strong enough. I groan my way up the stairs, feeble as a sick dog. When I'm settled in bed, she draws the covers over me, and dimly I'm grateful because I'm bone-shaking cold. After she feeds me a couple of Advil, she leaves the room. I start shivering like it's February, not July.

Was I crying when Floyd was pounding me? I'll never know.

The creak of hinges stirs me from a stupor that's part sleep, part plain old endurance. I open my good eye. Cassie edges into the room, closing the door behind her. She climbs up on the bed and burrows into me. Muscles in my chest go into spasm. My breath hisses between my teeth. She's warm though, and a stray thought drifts through my brain ... maybe I need her as bad as she needs me.

Me need Cassie? *Your brain's addled, Brick. Too many blows to the head.*

We lie still. Endurance isn't a pastime I recommend. Then she whispers, "You okay?"

"Mmm ... You were a good girl to go upstairs, Cassie."

A sob hiccups in her chest. "If I'd been watching *Nemo*, I'd have heard him coming."

"With AC/DC cranked up so loud? Nah." Even though every word hurts, I persevere. "It wasn't your fault. It's never your fault."

"Never ever?"

"It's his fault. Always."

"You hit him."

"Yeah ... I hit him." I feel, deep down, a flicker of pride.

Which is followed by a terror that drenches me in sweat. I *hit* Floyd? There's disobedience and there's insanity. If ever I should run away from home, it's now.

I can't even lift my head off the pillow.

Cassie has to be hungry. But she doesn't complain. Eventually we doze off. When I wake up, she's gone, the crows are cutting a racket in the trees behind the house, and the sun's shining. Thought it was supposed to rain ... Marigold might get those petunias planted today.

Cassie left Rover for me. His shiny black skunk-eyes are staring at me. *Okay, buddy, I got me a black eye too.*

I could buy her a teddy bear. A white one with a pink bow around its neck.

4.1 [all the comforts of home]

THE DAY goes like this:

Take a leak.

Look in the mirror. Wish I hadn't. Right eye black, shading to maroon. Lip split, cheek swollen.

Teeth still attached.

Have a shower. Loosens me up some. My chest—my skinny chest—looks like somebody planted purple petunias all over it.

Take anti-inflammatories. Maximum dose.

Ask Cassie to bring ice packs and toast upstairs. Eat the toast. More peanut butter in her hair than on the bread.

Worry about her.

Stumble into Opal's office to use her phone even though it's her Personal Space and therefore off-limits. Come to think of it, not even Floyd comes in here.

Sun streams through the open window, filmy curtains swaying in the breeze. Rainbows from the crystals she's hung from the window frames wander over the far wall. Books, embroidered cushions, polished pine floor; and everywhere chunks of jade, rose quartz, and amethyst. How can the woman who arranged all this with such care treat her only son like he's a hole in the landscape?

Eight years ago. A psychic fair comes to town. Opal (then known as Audrey) can't get a sitter, so she drags me along. At first I enjoy myself. The tables are spread with purple satin that glitters with gold stars and crescent moons. Polished stones gleam in brass bowls. Incense burns in little curls of smoke and scent.

Audrey doesn't want to leave; her cheeks are flushed and her eyes glazed. By now, a couple of hours have passed and I'm tired and whiny. She tells me to go sit by the wall because she has an appointment to have her palm read by the woman in the flowing blue dress.

When it's over, she's ablaze with excitement. She walks right past me and pushes open the exit door without even checking to see if I'm tagging along behind her.

I was as scared of her that day as I am of Floyd every day.

Once I'm living in Halifax, things will quiet down here. No more beatings, because I'm the one who triggers Floyd. Cassie won't have to worry about the go-upstairs command anymore, and she'll stop having nightscares. She'll be okay.

Not great, given Floyd and Opal. But okay.

Some of the tension seeps out of me. I sit down on the couch, which is so soft that I lean back, closing my good eye, wishing I could stay here forever.

Opal's wind chimes jingle and sing.

I fall asleep. Wake up and realize it's twelve thirty. Time has passed. Time has a habit of doing this. Today I'm all for it.

Sluggish as a bear in winter, I key in Rolf's number. He picks up the phone. Must be his lunch break. "It's Brick," I say. "I'm not feeling so good. Could we do the money-thing last of the week?"

"Flu's going around."

"Fell off the ATV." Hastily I add, "Cassie wasn't on it."

"How about Friday, then? I'm on days—come over at noon."

I hang up just as Opal marches into the office; she must have heard my voice. I mumble, "Thanks for stopping him, Opal."

She stands still, her long skirt swirling around her ankles. "You don't ever want to take him on. Not Floyd."

I lever myself to my feet and wait until the rainbows stop swooping and diving. "He's gotta stop beating up on me in front of Cassie."

Her mouth tightens. "Things are really rough at work right now."

"It terrifies her! You have to talk to him."

"I can try. But there are no guarantees with Floyd."

At least she's listening; Floyd losing his cool shook her up. Knowing I don't mean it, I say, "I'll go to the cops if he lays a finger on me when Cassie's in the same room."

"You don't want to do that, either. We'll watch over her."

"We? You planning on staying home with her? Or taking her with you when you go out?"

"I can't do that! My healing work, it's confidential." She glances at herself in the mirror. "I have to center myself. Off you go."

Off I go. Obedience should be my middle name, not Thaddeus. Brickson was Opal's maiden name, Thaddeus was Floyd's father. They couldn't even come up with a name that belonged only to me.

Downstairs, I lower myself into the nearest chair in the kitchen, head on the table, and wish it was tomorrow. A week from tomorrow.

More time passes. I heat up a can of Alphagettis for Cassie. Smell nearly makes me heave.

Opal comes downstairs. "I have appointments in town, then Floyd and I are having supper together," she says. "I'll try and talk to him. Afterward, he has a meeting and I'm doing palm readings in Hilchey Point."

I'd sigh with relief except it'd hurt too much.

Sleep some more. Watch *Sesame Street*. Oscar grumping in his garbage can.

Oh no. It's recycling day. My job to put it out by the road.

Surely today Floyd would have done it for me.

Send Cassie to check. The green bin's sitting beside the garage.

The truck's due in fifteen minutes. Docker's always on time.

The bin is way too big for Cassie.

If it's not emptied ... let's not go there.

4.2 [white knight]

THIRTEEN MINUTES later, we reach the end of the driveway, me wheeling the bin, Cassie and Rover tagging along for company. Docker's just pulling up in his big green and white truck. He's alone today; the other guy must be sick. I push the bin the last couple of feet, turn my back, and try not to stagger. Step-by-step, I shuffle toward the house.

The brakes squeal, the cab door slams. Docker catches up with me easy, since running's not on my agenda. "What happened?"

"Fell off the ATV," I say. "Onto some rocks—smashed up my face."

"He did it," Cassie says.

She knows and I know that *he* means Floyd. Docker doesn't know. Pushing words past the pain in my jaw, I say, "That's right,

Cassie, it wasn't the ATV's fault. I was the one driving it. Forgot my helmet."

Cassie jams her thumb in her mouth, a habit I thought she'd outgrown. "Don't pay her any mind," I add, "she's cranky because I put a dent in the ATV. That Disney movie about the cars—she thinks our ATV should've been the big star, not Lightning McQueen, because our ATV is what takes us to MacTaggart's and the library." And when am I going to quit running off at the mouth?

My split lip is bleeding. I dab at it.

Docker gazes at me in silence. Gray hair, a nose that looks like it was broken long ago, steady brown eyes. He says quietly, "Did someone beat you up?"

If he twigs to Floyd, guess who'll be the next corpse in the Dead Zone? Clinging to the lid of the green bin, I say desperately, "The river trail's rough and I wasn't watching what I was doing."

"He did it," Cassie says. "He's a meanie."

I give her a look that would stop a rutting moose dead in his tracks. "Okay, okay," I say sulkily. "It wasn't the ATV. Snyder McIsaac caught me down by the river. Him and his gang."

Docker's eyes move from me to Cassie. He says to her, no expression in his voice, "Want to watch while I dump your bin?"

Her thumb leaves her mouth. She nods.

He could at least smile at her.

After he wheels the green bin to the hoist, he climbs in the cab; hoist-plus-bin groan their way upward. Cassie watches, big-eyed, as the black maw of the truck swallows our leftovers.

The hoist lowers the bin. Docker jumps to the ground. "I'll push the bin back up the driveway."

"I can do it!"

He takes the handles and adjusts his pace to mine. I do my best to walk natural, but the road's wavering and twice I have to grab the bin, blood pounding in my ears. As he lines the bin up carefully by the garage door, he says, "Have you seen a doctor?"

"Nah."

It's as much as I can do not to flinch when he takes me by the elbow. But he's only steering me toward the door, supporting me so I don't fall flat on my kisser. He says, "I want you to do something for me."

I sit down on the step, breathing shallow, waiting for the line of trees to settle.

"On the weekend, come to the mall and visit my dojo—the place where I teach karate."

I'd drop my jaw, except it's too sore. "Why?"

"It would be a good discipline for you to have."

"I got no use for that stuff."

"You won't know until you try."

I say sullenly, "All summer I babysit Cassie."

"Bring her along. I have a play area for little kids. How about two p.m. on Saturday?"

"There were four of them! What good is karate then?"

Docker doesn't bother answering. "Bye, Cassie. See you, Brick," he says and jogs down the driveway. Jogs like it's his natural pace, no wasted motion.

"Cassie," I say, dabbing at my lip again, "you're not to tell anyone, anyone at all, that Floyd beats up on me. If you do it again, I'll never take you back to the library. Or MacTaggart's."

She sucks in her breath. "But it was a big Bang-up."

"He'd be real angry if he found out I'd blabbed on him."

Floyd's anger she understands. "Okay." Then the thumb goes back in her mouth.

"Let's go inside," I say.

Six months ago. School's back after the Christmas break. Behind the gym, when Brian Colpitts won't hand over his new Atlanta Braves ball cap, I try roughing him up. But he's always just out of reach, dodging, deflecting my fists with his arm, landing kicks so fast I don't see them coming. Kicks that sting. Power behind them. Other kids are starting to gather, so I take off, looking as though the whole thing is nothing to do with me.

Later, I learn that Brian's taking karate.

Lie down.

For supper, make hot dogs, which Cassie eats in front of the TV. Supervise her slopping around in the tub, so what if she forgets the soap.

Oh, the Places You'll Go! is downstairs.

Recite her favorite picture book instead, about a stripy cat and how it finds a good home.

Then I do something I've never done before. I lean over and give her a kiss. On the top of her head.

Her hair tickles my nose.

I say, "G'night, Cassie. Night, Rover. See you in the morning." That's regular, at least.

She says sleepily, "Horton's a happy elephant."

I leave the bedside lamp on low, because of her nightscares, close her door, clean up the bathroom, which looks as though a force-three hurricane passed through, go to my room, close the door, swallow four Advil—who cares what the maximum dose is—and very carefully lie down on the bed.

I survived the day.

Just because Marigold kissed Cassie doesn't mean I have to. First thing you know, she'll expect it. Every night.

After I leave home, no one will kiss her. All of a sudden, the reality of Cassie here without me sinks in. No one to read to her or cook chicken fingers. No one to take her places on the ATV and choose the library books she likes. The thought of her alone and lonely in this crappy old house hurts me deeper than my sore ribs.

But leaving here when I'm sixteen—it's nonnegotiable.

We've got months, we'll figure something out.

I lie still, waiting for the Advil to kick in. How about you speed-read the following boring description of a boring guy's boring room. Rust bedspread, single bed, pine floor. One window crowded with branches, leaves on in summer, leaves off in winter. A small closet with clothes neatly hung in a row; bureau with tidy drawers; wooden chair that's too small for me; digital clock with the usual red numbers that jump from minute to minute. Old-fashioned clocks go around in circles that represent continuity, also known as the endless—pointless?—Cycle of Life. The

Advil must be working. I hear myself being profound.

No desk, no bookshelves, library books on top of the bureau beside the boom box. No photos, no posters of rock stars, no *Playboy* under the pillow. Take no hostages, leave no clues. My bedroom has exactly one secret, the stash of bills under the mattress, which is not the hiding place of a profound thinker.

I'm drifting off to sleep. If I believed in God instead of Floyd, I'd say thank you.

4.3 [pay dirt]

SUMMARY OF the next three days: Technicolor bruises from forehead to shin; lip that scabs over, bleeds when I eat, scabs over; headache that finally goes away on Thursday.

I don't want to leave the property looking like an amateur oil painting and, besides, it rains for two solid days. So Cassie and I overdose on TV, which means I sit through *Treehouse, The Backyardigans, Imagination Movers,* and *Sesame Street,* listening to her give Rover a running commentary on the action.

The TV is a sixty-inch flat screen HD, nothing but the best for Floyd.

≈

I KISS Cassie good night on Tuesday, Wednesday, and Thursday. I sneak a peak at her on Wednesday night before closing her door. She's smiling to herself like she's happy, and if that's all it takes, I guess I can manage one measly kiss per day.

The good news? Floyd is working on a jigsaw puzzle. Nope, you're not losing it. Jigsaw puzzle is what I said.

The guitar is for when he's relaxed. To get relaxed, he does jigsaws, spreading the pieces on an old card table. Difficult jigsaws with over one thousand pieces that he orders online, some of them circular or oval, some made of wood. I'm all in favor of him lowering his stress level.

Still, I keep Cassie out of Floyd's way. I keep myself out of Floyd's way. For three days. Unfortunately, I slip up on Thursday evening when I drop a glass and it shatters on the floor. Floyd's into the kitchen like a slapshot to the net.

"That glass belonged to my father—it's irreplaceable. You broke it on purpose, didn't you?"

Trying not to tremble, I say, "It was an accident."

He bounces on the balls of his feet, his eyes locked onto mine. "You're lying."

I can't help it. I take a step back. Glass snaps under my heel. "S-sorry."

From the living room, the crowd screams as someone scores. Soccer, rugby, what do I care as long as it distracts him? Obviously he hasn't forgotten that I attacked him, swore at him, and made Opal lose her cool, thereby humiliating him—the ultimate sin.

"Clean it up," he says, and marches out of the room.

My knees don't want to hold me up. I stumble into the pantry to fetch the broom and dustpan.

Okay, let's try and gain some historical perspective (a phrase used frequently by Mrs. Baldwin, history teacher, grades seven and eight):

```
Josef Stalin (1879-1953): responsible for the deaths
    of approximately 25 million (approximately ...
    means no one bothered—or was left—to keep track).
Vlad III (ca 1431-1476)(the original Dracula—
    see, reading broadens your horizons): impaled
    thousands of men, women and children.
Popé (ca 1630-1690): led a rebellion against the
    Spanish conquistadors, then became a brutal
    tyrant himself.
Phraates IV (ruled Parthia ca 37-32 BC): killed his
    father to gain the throne.
```

FRIDAY NOON, I lift Cassie on the ATV. Since I've already told Rolf that I fell off it, I'll have to stick to that particular lie and hope he and Docker don't compare notes.

As I fasten her helmet, I say, "Remember what I told you? You won't tell Rolf, Marigold, Tully, or Caramel that Floyd beat me up. I fell off the ATV down by the river and hurt my face on the rocks. Got it?"

"Telling lies is bad," she says. I bet she's quoting from *The Backyardigans*.

"Usually. But when you live with Floyd, telling lies is the only way to go."

I turn on the ignition and we drive away, every jounce and bounce grating my teeth. The power truck's parked in Rolf's driveway. The house looks great, and Marigold has planted— guess what—orange, red, and yellow marigolds in the window boxes, along with smudgy little blue flowers.

"Pretty," Cassie says.

Caramel bounds into the yard and she forgets the flowers. Rolf comes out on the step. He blinks. "Fell off your ATV, is that what you said?"

"Down by the river. Landed on some rocks." Funny, I don't like lying to him.

He doesn't look altogether convinced. "You sure did a num- ber on yourself, fella ... that's what helmets are for. Be prepared, Marigold will fuss."

Inside, Marigold is shredding lettuce for a salad. She glances up as I walk in the kitchen, and for a moment she looks like the one who was hit in the face. "What happened?"

I trot out the ATV lie again.

"Oh. Oh, I see," she says. She looks relieved. "I thought per- haps it was Snyder McIsaac."

Rolf says sharply, "Was it?"

"No way," I say. "My own fault, I wasn't wearing a helmet."

As if she can't help herself, Marigold touches her fingertips to my black eye, asking if it still hurts. Then she fetches a cream with something called Arnica in it, and dabs it on the bruises. By the time she's finished, my face is red from more than Floyd's fists, especially with Tully watching from the sidelines, her gaze as cold as the bay in winter.

I was too busy with Marigold to notice Tully's reaction when she first saw my face. I don't think she believes the ATV story, though—she's likely hoping all the guys in my grade ganged up and beat the tar out of me.

We eat fish chowder and homemade tea biscuits, still warm, followed by strawberry-rhubarb pie with ice cream, me worrying the whole time that my lip will drip blood on the plate. Rolf pushes back his chair.

"Gotta go—we had a call out Swamp Road. Brick, here's your money, and remember what I said about a reference."

As he hands me the envelope, he's smiling. I tuck it in my pocket. "Thanks."

It's Tully's job to clean up the dishes. Marigold says, "If you want to go to the bank, Brick, why don't you leave Cassie here and pick her up on your way back?"

"I can play with Caramel," Cassie says.

I park behind the mall. The envelope contains twenty-dollar bills, ten of them. Rolf scrawled on the back of the envelope, *For painting and scraping*.

Sitting on the ATV, I finger the little wad of bills. He valued my work enough to pay me, generous pay; and he said he'd give me a reference.

If only I could tell Marigold and Rolf the truth about Floyd.

I put the bills back in the envelope. I was figuring on $150 max. I'm going to treat myself to a new set of headphones for my boom box.

Eyes front, quick (well, not so quick) march to The Source, buy them, and out again. Phew. I adjust my dark glasses, pull the

brim of my ball cap farther down over my face, and trudge past
the GM dealership.

*Ten years ago? How old am I when Floyd first takes me there—four?
I'm wearing new plaid shorts with the crease still in them. He wouldn't
let me put on my Tonka T-shirt because a Tonka isn't a GM. He
tells me the names of all the cars in the showroom—Blazer, Sunfire,
Cavalier, and Camaro—and I rattle them off after him. The other
salesmen laugh. Someone gives me a red balloon, someone else puts
money in a machine and out comes an orange ball of bubblegum.
I say thank you. Floyd is proud of me.*

Although it's only a five-minute walk to the bank on Main Street,
it feels like five miles. People on the sidewalk glance at my face,
look away fast. Same holds true in the bank, especially after I take
off the dark glasses. The teller is pretty; she's wearing a tight green
sweater. I'm surprised that sweater made it past the manager. Then
again, if he's a guy, maybe not.

I say I want to open a savings account and push the money
at her. Two hundred dollars minus the headset, plus the stash,
which amounts to $418 in small bills. I don't tell her the latter
has been stolen over a period of five years. Some of it was kids'
lunch money, but mostly it's from Opal.

I keep back fifteen dollars to buy Cassie a white teddy
bear.

The teller says I can't have a bank card without parental con-
sent. Superpolite, I say the money's for saving, not spending. She
glances at my black eye (actually red, pink, purple, and yellow),

passes me the little blue bankbook and says, unconvincingly, "Of course."

I walk out. I'll hide the bankbook in my room. No worries now that Floyd will find my stash.

4.4 [book learning]

ON THE way back to the ATV, I pass The Laughing Loon, the bookstore Glenn's father owns. He added a café where you can sit on the deck in summer, sip your iced tea with lemon, and watch the tide go in and out. Tourists go for that kind of thing.

Glenn is sitting on the step. My dark glasses are back on, but they're useless for a split lip. He says, "You took on Snyder McIsaac."

"Not likely."

"You lost an argument with a bouncer."

"Troubles enough without adding booze to the mix."

His lashes flicker; I didn't mean to sound so bitter. He says, "You fired a rock at a bear cub whose mother objected."

His dad's inside the store, so he knows he's safe. How weird must that be. I give him a skewed smile, which is all I can manage, and keep walking.

The library is across the road from the bookstore. If there's anyplace I feel at home, it's the library.

The theme of the week is Adolescent Self-Help. I'm nearly past the rack when two titles spring out at me. One's about teenage anxiety, the other about bullying in schools. I lift them fast and go straight to the automated checkout. The machine *thunks* as it registers each title. I pull out the date slip, tuck the books under my arm, titles inward, and I'm out the door.

As usual, the bakery smells of chocolate chip cookies.

I can't walk any faster or my muscles will seize up; memories of Kendra slam into me like Floyd's fists. Kendra Ryan at Happy Whale Daycare ... for the first four years of my life, I thought she was my real mother, and Audrey/Opal was the babysitter.

Kendra baked chocolate chip cookies every Monday. When I was six, Mrs. Sanger replaced her, and from then on we ate packaged cookies from Sobeys. Chocolate chip cookies always taste to me of loss.

Which has never stopped me from eating them, cramming them in my mouth in the hopes they'll fill the gap Kendra left behind. Eight years have passed and it hasn't worked yet.

She never said goodbye.

I zip the books inside the carry-bag on the rear rack of the ATV, already regretting that I took them out, knowing they're going to nag at me the rest of the day.

THREE NEW jigsaws that arrived in the mail are sitting on the dining room table. I guess Opal must have opened the package.

They're reproductions of paintings, which seems a bizarre choice for Mr. Macho MacAvoy until I look them over and realize each one is a major challenge. Particularly Monet's *Waterlilies*, where most of the puzzle is the pale turquoise surface of the pond.

Guaranteed to keep Floyd out of my face.

How to figure out Floyd's moods—you could say that's been the major puzzle of my life. Here's what I've put together:

```
A.  Johnny Cash on the guitar, anything from
    "Accidentally on Purpose" to "Straight A's in
    Love." Mood: terrific.
B.  Jigsaw puzzles, the more complicated the better.
    Mood: somewhat less than terrific but still
    pretty darn good.
C.  TV: wrestling, boxing and Ultimate Fighting.
    Mood: can go either way (guaranteed bad if he's
    interrupted).
D.  Beat on your son. Mood: from extraordinarily bad
    to terrific, bring on Johnny Cash, "Flesh and
    Blood."
```

As soon as Cassie's tucked in for the night, I go to my room, close the door, and take the anxiety book out of the drawer where I hid it under my socks. I'm a teenager, so part of the title fits. But anxiety? Is that just a highbrow word for fear?

Fear is what I live with, fear that sometimes hibernates and sometimes claws me like a grizzly. I skim through the chapters, bypassing sexuality, dating, peer pressure, intercourse, and eating habits. But the section on parents pulls me in like it's quicksand. Parents who drink or do drugs, parents who don't parent but foist the job on their kids, parents who abuse their kids sexually or physically. Mouth dry, I read on.

Actual teenagers tell their stories, guys and girls. This makes it worse. But the advice is what caps it. Leave home. Don't wait until the damage is permanent. Get help. Talk to a relative. Tell someone in a position of authority.

I can see me trotting into the RCMP detachment and fingering Floyd, Head Salesman at the GM dealership on Main Street and Treasurer of the Chamber of Commerce. Just the thought of it makes me sweat in places you don't want to know about. Although now I have another name for it. Anxiety.

I shove the book back under my socks. Because my brain's jittering, I can't settle to sleep, so eventually I pull out the other book, the one about bullying in schools. In case you're wondering, we've had sessions in assembly on bullying. Several, I guess. I'm guessing because I'm a straight-A student in the most valuable lesson school can teach you, which is how to tune out.

I read the blurb and the author's credentials. This book isn't on my junior-high reading list with a 250-word report due by Monday, five points deducted for lateness. I could drop it in the Return slot tomorrow and who'd know?

The first chapter defines bullying. *Bullying involves the abuse of power, verbally or physically, by one person or a group. It can be low-key or severe, one-time or repetitive.*

I don't do groups, and verbal's a waste of time.

Other words jump from the page. *Intentional. Unjustified.* Phrases and sentences snag my eyes. *The bully hurts/humiliates/dominates the victim, often with enjoyment. The victim is usually smaller or in some way helpless. Typically, the bully denies what he's doing, both to others and to himself.*

No wonder I used to tune out in assembly.

I skip ahead, riffling through the pages. *The bully is often socially isolated, doesn't feel shame, and lacks empathy.* Does the guy who wrote this book know me?

The truth creeps through my veins cold as a winter snake.

I'm a bully.

Me, Brick MacAvoy. A full-fledged, genuine, go-for-broke bully. I don't just bug kids, or hassle them, or pick on them. I *bully* them.

Their faces parade through my brain: Lorne Meisner, Gary Sanger, Lucas Donovan, Samson Donovan, Billy Gottrich, Glenn Semple. Kicks, punches, wedgies, wrist burns, threats piled on threats. Wary faces. Terrified faces, tight with pain. Kids whimpering, sobbing, even, on occasion, screaming. Although not, of course, Glenn.

I'm no better than Snyder McIsaac. Except I travel alone.

I rip open the packaging on my new headphones, plug them in, turn the volume up high, and wallow in AC/DC.

"Dirty Deeds Done Dirt Cheap."

5.1 [AQ]

WHEN I wake up in the middle of the night, the pillow is on the floor and the sheet's twisted around my neck as if I've been trying to strangle myself in my sleep.

Another revelation is straddling my chest, heavier than Snyder. If bullying is about the abuse of power by hurting and humiliating someone smaller than you, then Floyd's a prime suspect. Nothing he likes better than to make the tears pour down my face.

Floyd's a bully and I'm a bully. Like father, like son. Blood is thicker than water. The reason clichés hang around is because they're true.

I slam the door on my thoughts, grab my pillow, and pound it back into shape. No way am I a younger version of Floyd. I'm out of my mind to even contemplate anything so far-out. So gross.

Another Dr. Seuss book that Cassie likes is *Oh, the Thinks You Can Think!* Right now, I wish I could think my way out the side door and down the road to the bus stop in Hilchey Bay, where a bus would be waiting to drive me to Halifax. Why stop there? Think myself to Vancouver. Mongolia. Outer space. Anywhere, as long as I leave the whole damn lot of them behind.

FLOYD ISN'T on the Saturday shift today. Cassie is standing by the sink and Opal is in the pantry, yawning as she measures the coffee and dumps it in the filter. "I'm taking Floyd his coffee in bed," she says.

Well, aren't you the clever one. "I'm leaving for the day," I say.

"Take Cassie with you."

"I don't want to."

"Brick, take Cassie with you."

No use arguing with that tone of voice.

Cassie is staring at me, her eyes huge, Rover glued to her chest. "You leaving me home?"

"We'll go to the beach."

She lets Rover fall to his usual position, nose to the floor. Her whole face brightens. "I can wear my new swimsuit."

I ask Opal for lunch money, bundle Cassie on the ATV along with her plastic buckets and spades, and take her to the Hilchey Bay Beach. I bought the new swimsuit back in June; Opal gave me fifteen dollars, the swimsuit (green ruffles, pink stripes) was on sale, eight ninety-nine, the change went to the stash.

The beach is a long curve of pale sand that stretches all the way from Collings Head to Hilchey Point. It draws tourists in droves every summer, which helps keep Hilchey Bay more or less alive.

Usually the waves kind of hypnotize me, one crash-landing after another—so do the shorebirds that zigzag like little gray robots near the waterline. Today, I just stare out to sea. Horizon knife-sharp. You can see why they used to believe you could fall off the edge.

The gulls are screaming Floyd's name.

The reason I can't get away from him is because he's taken up residence. Birds of a feather, that's Floyd and me.

Fidgety as the surf, keeping my shirt on so my bruises won't frighten the tourists, I help Cassie build a sand castle decorated with dried seaweed and clamshells. Kendra used to take the older kids to the beach on sunny days in summer, all of us linked together by a fat yellow rope we clutched in our left hands. She'd build big towers of sand with a walled track around the outside so you could roll a ball from the peak to the moat, where it would plop into the water. I loved doing that.

Cassie's happy with the castle we've built. Then I notice two of the Donovans, Lucas and his younger brother Samson, flying a kite near the dunes.

If I could rip that kite out of their hands, send it sailing over the ocean—or, better still, plunging into the waves, struts broken, string tangled—I'd feel better.

My anxiety would plunge along with the kite.

An acronym drops into my mind neat as can be. AQ. Anxiety Quotient. My brain runs with it.

```
ASSIGNMENT 1:      draw a graph.
Horizontal Axis:   number of days since Floyd laid
                   into me
Vertical Axis:     AQ
Result:            straight line angled upward at 45°.
ASSIGNMENT 2:      correlate AQ with bullying.
Result:            0 bullying until AQ hits the
                   mid-range (unless there's a golden
                   opportunity, such opportunity often
                   related to Glenn Semple), and then
                   1 or 2 episodes ASAP.


Keep It Simple, Stupid. Pressure builds as I wait for
Floyd to make his move. Bullying lets off pressure.
Save graph paper. Be good to the environment.
```

The beach comes back into focus. Don't know why it took me so long to figure all this out; my IQ's well up the scale for a guy from the backwoods, and I've always been good at math. Too bad my AQ's high as well. Still, Anxiety Quotient sounds classier than Fear Quotient.

Poor Brick, he's feeling anxious today ... Maybe all I'm doing is making excuses for being a bully. And if the thought of turning into Floyd terrifies me more than Floyd himself, then I should be ignoring the Donovans' kite.

The sand is hot under my heels. Cassie pads back and forth with her bucket, trying to keep water in the moat even though it keeps soaking in. I didn't bring the self-help (who are they kidding?) books to the beach. Instead, I read about some guys stranded in a rowboat off an Arctic island in winter—cannibalism suspected—and keep an eye on Cassie as she splashes in the waves. Once she's dried off, we have lunch at McDonald's. Cow meat.

5.2 [*kihon, kata, kumite*]

I DON'T want to go to Docker Lonergan's dojo. But if I don't, he's just as likely to truck me there on garbage day; the way he looks at you brings *persistent* to mind.

Lonergan's Karate, All Levels is next to the pet store, with a plain glass door and the kind of windows you can't see through. Cassie, of course, wants to go to the pet store and/or back to the beach. I push on the glass door.

A buzzer goes off as we step inside a small office. Docker walks in. He's wearing thick white pajamas with wide legs and long sleeves, a ratty black belt knotted around his waist. Bare feet. He looks bigger than usual.

"Hey, Brick," he says. He's noticed me staring at his outfit. Plucking at his sleeve, he adds, "It's called a *gi*," and leads us inside.

The *dojo*—the word comes easier now I'm here—is basically a gym with a hardwood floor and mirrors along two sides. At the front hang five long white banners with wiggly black characters on them. A black-and-white photo of a stern old Japanese guy keeps them company. No other equipment.

Before I step onto the hardwood, Docker says, "Bare feet only, Brick. Cassie, same goes for you."

While I'm taking off my sneakers, he bows to the old guy. Then he says, "Cassie, come see the toys. You'll like them."

She stays put. She's in shy mode.

I've already realized Docker's face doesn't show what's going on behind it. But when he reaches down and takes her by the hand, he looks like he's having a tooth drilled minus anesthetic.

Then he's back to impassive. He says, "There's a play store with little boxes and cans of food, and a cash register with plastic money."

Her face lights up and she trots alongside him like the angel she isn't. The play store is in a small room off the dojo.

I leave my dark glasses tucked in my socks. From a distance, my mirrored face looks like a drunk went berserk with a makeup kit. My bare soles feel cold on the polished floor.

A woman comes up behind me, takes off her sandals, and walks into the dojo. Same rig as Docker but with a brown belt, her hair yanked back into an elastic. "Hi, Docker," she says, then smiles at me. Doesn't even blink at my multicolored face.

"Brick, this is Michaela. Michaela, Brick MacAvoy." She smiles again. Ordinary is how she looks.

Docker keeps talking. "Karate's an ancient Japanese form of self-defense, Brick. You learn fundamental moves called *kihon*, series of moves called *kata*, and you learn how to spar, *kumite*." He spells out these words as he goes. "The purpose is so you can defend yourself if you're attacked."

Defend myself against Floyd? You joke.

"It's not a form of aggression. Ever."

Is he warning me against perfecting my bullying skills? Does he even know I'm a bully?

"Once we've warmed up," he says, "we'll demonstrate a few blocks, punches, and kicks, and do the *kata* you'd learn as a white belt. Then we'll spar."

I stand with my back to the mirror while they do exercises to warm up. They're both fit, I'll give them that. Before they start any of the fancy stuff that begins with *k*, they bow to each other. Docker says, straight-faced, "You always show respect for your opponent."

Me bowing to Floyd, that'd go over big.

Michaela punches, Docker blocks. Docker punches, Michaela blocks. Although the punches are so fast you can barely see them, and although slippery Brian Colpitts comes to mind, I figure the whole thing's like a ritual. Preplanned.

They do the *kata* in unison, bare feet slapping the floor, fists snapping out at empty air. Twice they give this almighty yell, makes me just about jump out of my sweats.

Their faces are intent, the same way Floyd looks when he's laying into me. I take a deep breath past the pain in my ribs. Wonder what would happen if Docker took on Floyd.

Docker says, "Now we'll demonstrate free-sparring, *jiyu kumite*."

He and Michaela bow again, he calls out something in Japanese, and they go at it. Fast, furious, focused. Blocks, elbow strikes, kicks high and low that are—I admit it—impressive, even though they all stop just short of contact. When she tumbles him over her shoulder to the floor, my eyes nearly pop out. She's four inches shorter than him. He whirls on one foot and kicks her ear. She lands a punch to his chest as the side of his foot zaps her knee.

Everything happens so fast I'm breathless. When they stop, there's an instant of perfect stillness before they bow and walk over to me. They're sweating, both of them, chests heaving. For a split second I have this image of me dumping Floyd on the kitchen floor, standing over him with one of those victory yells.

I say to Michaela, "How long did it take you to learn that?"

"Four years."

I'll be long gone by then. Docker says casually, "We also teach some basic self-defense moves. Against the sleeper hold, for example—maybe you've seen it used in Ultimate Fighting."

He grapples Michaela from behind, wrapping an arm around her throat. Instantly she tucks her chin against her chest, drags down on his arm, kicks his shin, and twists free.

He grasps her by both wrists. She steps toward him, leans back, whips her hands up and out, and stamps on his instep—except it isn't there.

She says, dead serious, "I can break the bones in his foot that way."

I don't want to be impressed.

Docker says, "Thanks a lot, Michaela."

"My pleasure, Sensei." She bows to the old guy in the photo and pads out the door.

"Does that give you the general idea, Brick?"

"I can't do any of that!"

"I can teach you enough so that never again will your face look like ham on a hook. At least not with a single opponent. But I don't want you having unrealistic expectations—this isn't the movies. You're young, so you don't yet have the upper body strength for punches that'll accomplish much. It can take years to perfect those. Karate will give you focus and balance, though, and improve your speed. And I always teach elbow and knee strikes, along with kicks, for self-defense."

So he must have believed me when I told him Snyder and his gang beat up on me. As long as it stays that way, I'm safe. "I gotta go."

Docker says calmly, "You're in no shape to start anything for a few more days. On Wednesday I'll pick you up around four thirty and we'll get started. Wear sweatpants, a T-shirt, and sneakers."

I jam my hands in my pockets. "How much is this gonna cost me?"

"For now, it's on the house."

"I don't get it—what's in it for you?"

"Next time you have a tussle with your ATV, you'll come out on top."

Very funny. "So I'm a charity case?"

"Brick, anyone who joins the dojo gets a few free lessons before they have to pay. Let's just see how it goes, and we can talk money later."

"I'll let you know by Tuesday if I decide not to come."

Cassie isn't ready to be separated from the plastic cash register. Docker says, "You can play with it again another day, Cassie."

Like I said, persistent.

5.3 [pride and prejudice]

CASSIE DRAGS her feet all the way out of the mall, and because she's pissing me off, I'm not paying full attention. As we come around the corner of Shoppers Drug Mart, the four guys who are standing around the ATV turn their heads. Snyder McIsaac and three of his goons.

Where's Docker when you need him?

Snyder lifts his shades, studies my face. Three or four more trips to McDonald's and he'll have a double chin. "Ain't you the pretty sight," he says. "Babysitting your little sister again? How cute is that."

Cassie clutches my thigh. Snyder's buddies loosely circle us. Repeat Appearance of Chinless MacAvoy. "We forgot something at Shoppers," I mumble. "See ya."

"Not so fast," Snyder says. "You got money on you?"

The fifteen dollars for Cassie's white teddy bear is in my wallet. I wasn't in the mood for Zellers after the dojo, so I didn't mention it to her. "Nah," I say, "we left a package on the counter."

Snyder signals. The three others elbow into me. Cassie starts to whimper. My sentiments exactly. One of them grabs for my wallet, knocking into Cassie, whose whimper turns into a howl. I stoop to pick her up, get kneed in the kidneys and grunt with pain. Too soon after the last beating, that's all I can think as I hoist her in my arms and jam her face into my shirt.

Someone punches me from behind. Nearly rocks me off my feet.

So loud it makes me jump, a horn starts blaring the rhythm of "O Canada." My head swings around.

Tully Langille, astride her bike, is squeezing the rubber bulb of the Klaxon on her handlebars: one note only, the sound somewhere between a snort and a fart. She switches to "Here Comes the Bride."

Heads turn in the parking lot. An SUV stops, the driver peering at us.

Snyder says through gritted teeth, "See you later, MacAvoy," then lumbers away, his three sidekicks trailing him like the tail of a comet.

As he passes Tully, he says, "Watch yourself, slut."

Tully gives a rude toot on the horn. I pat Cassie on the back, my heart still racketing in my chest. "It's okay, Cassie. They've gone." Tears are swimming in her eyes, although she's doing her best to blink them back. I don't have a Kleenex.

Tully wheels over, pulls a tattered tissue from her pocket, and offers it. "So, Brick, how does it feel to have someone throwing rocks at you?"

"Gee," I say, "a metaphor."

Her eyes narrow, mean as Snyder's. "Here's a noun for you—empathy. Try it on for size."

"That why you horned in on Snyder?" I don't want to say, *That why you came to my rescue?* Too humiliating.

"Gee," she says, "a pun. I came to your rescue because I like Cassie." She glares at me. "You didn't fall off your ATV a few days ago—Snyder and his gang caught up with you. Is that what you do in your spare time, go looking for fights?"

I zip my lip. Better that Tully thinks Snyder is responsible than have her guessing the truth. I squeeze Cassie's arm so she'll keep her mouth shut.

Tully's gaze hardens. "No," she says, "you wouldn't pick a fight with someone bigger than you. So it must be d-r-u-g-s ... we don't want Cassie knowing what you're up to, do we? Did you double-cross them? They don't like it when kids knuckle in on their profits."

I hate being labeled a druggie. Especially by Tully Langille. But if it ever got out about Floyd—he'd kill me and ask questions afterward. My lip stays zipped.

"Funny," she says, "I'd have thought you were too smart to go the crack route."

"You spend a lot of time trying to figure me out?"

She flushes. "Why didn't you run the other way when you saw them near your ATV? Instead, you put Cassie in danger."

"Hindsight's twenty-twenty—gee, a cliché."

As Cassie gives a little hiccup, Tully's face softens. "Those guys aren't worth a single tear, Cassie," she says. "Take it from me."

She's wearing cutoffs, her legs smoothly muscled. Words force their way out.

"Be careful, Tully. Snyder doesn't like girls." I don't want to say *rape* in front of Cassie, which is what he's supposed to have done to Charlene Gottrich last fall, only she wouldn't press charges.

"Huh," Tully says, turns in a tight circle, pulls a wheelie, and peddles away.

BY NOW, you should have solved the following equation:

```
biceps, quads, and abs worth zilch + lousy hockey
player + no expensive toys, therefore no Facebook,
texting, Twittering, surfing, or handheld movies +
can't bring anyone home + surrogate parent for a
four-year-old who carries a stuffed skunk wherever
she goes + wouldn't spend money on a girl even
given the opportunity, such opportunity being as
likely to occur as a monsoon in the Gobi Desert +
bully + alleged drug-user = no girlfriend.
```

Sure I'm pissed off with Tully. But underneath the anger is hurt, and for some reason this makes me even angrier. So why did I bother with the stupid equation? It's not as though I want Tully Langille for my girlfriend; all the girls her age in Hilchey Bay outgrew wheelies years ago.

Something else. The thought of turning into Floyd gives me the creeps. But if Lorne Meisner was standing in front of me right now, would I be able to stop myself?

5.4 [hurt and humiliation]

WE GO home, where Cassie colors four red stick figures with huge hands and feet, brows like V's, then scrubs them out with her black crayon, the one that's worn to a stub.

Even if I was Brian Colpitts—or Docker Lonergan—I couldn't have dealt with four guys at once. Let's face it, the only guys I can deal with are Lorne-sized.

By the time I've finished the dishes, Cassie is upstairs, Opal's out, and Floyd's upset because boxing has been preempted by a softball championship. Softball and Floyd in the same sentence? He drops the remote on the table when he sees me in the doorway, and crosses the room.

His eyes bore into my skull. We stand like this for what feels like half an hour. The worst part, always, is the waiting.

He buries his fist in my hair. I throw my head back to prevent instant baldness. Bad move, the throat being one of the most vulnerable parts of the human anatomy. *One thing I'll grant you, Floyd—you've never kicked me in THE most vulnerable part.*

He says, real soft, "A week ago, you attacked me, kiddo—did you think I'd forgotten? Don't ever do it again."

"I won't," I croak.

He lifts me by the hair until I'm standing on my tiptoes. Until tears spurt from my eyes. His smile satisfied, he nods once or twice, then lets go so suddenly I nearly fall over.

There's fifty percent decent days, and there's five percent decent days.

WEDNESDAY MORNING and I'm standing at the bathroom sink in front of the mirror. My face is varying shades of yellow, which is only fitting for the biggest coward in five counties.

You know how the Mafia wires chunks of cement to the ankles of their victims before they toss them in the canal? That's how I feel when Floyd gets in my face, as though I'm hung with cement. It's how I feel with Snyder too.

No cement on Docker's feet and that's not because they were bare.

The only thing you have to fear is fear itself. Right on.

I didn't call Docker last night to cancel our date at the dojo.

It's like his feet know where they're standing and they've earned the right to stand there, and I'm talking garbage. It's Docker's job to haul the garbage away. When it comes to mine—

all the crap I've accumulated since Floyd started laying into me—good luck is all I can say.

Later, when Opal wanders downstairs in search of caffeine, I say, "I'm leaving Cassie with you at four thirty. I'll only be gone an hour or so."

Instantly, she's wide awake. "I have work to do."

"I could send an e-mail from the library to Floyd's boss, suggesting he ask Floyd what happened to his son's face."

"I don't think that's a good idea."

It's a suicidal idea. "Worth a try."

"Do I have to spell it out? He's edgy as a ripsaw these days."

"And I'm the two-by-four. Nice work when you can get it."

As she tosses her head, her crystal earrings shoot out splinters of violet and blue. "As it happens, I'm in my office this afternoon. Don't push your luck, Brick."

She stalks into the pantry. No cement on my feet with Opal because I don't give a rat's ass what she thinks of me. After all, what's she ever done for me?

You could say that stopping your husband from beating your son to a pulp is worth noting. But it's the first time she ever stopped him. That's equally worth noting.

5.5 ["King of the Road"]

AT 4:35 I climb into Docker's GM pickup. He says fitness is the first step and drives to Swamp Road, which is off #539.

I'll spare you the details, although I will say he talks to me as if I'm worth talking to, and his instructions are clear. We walk, jog, walk, jog, until I'm soaked in sweat. Then we lift weights. Then we stretch. Then he drives me back to his place.

Total traffic, one logging truck.

At least none of the Donovans drove by.

As he pockets the keys, he says, "Every second day, repeat that routine—and if you can afford it, buy some new running shoes, ones with good support. I'll loan you these weights until you're ready for a bigger set. Next Thursday, we'll go to the dojo."

So much for learning how to break the bones in his feet.

FRIDAY, MONDAY, and Wednesday, when I go through my routine, I discover I sort of like doing the weights—taking my time, remembering all Docker's instructions, gradually increasing the reps. I don't know which part of me hates the jogging more, my legs or my lungs. But I keep at it, don't ask me why, doing it in the morning after Floyd leaves for work and before Opal's ready to go out.

Side benefit: exercise lowers AQ.

Since the hair incident, Floyd's watched Ultimate Fighting every evening. What if he plans to practice on me?

THURSDAY, DOCKER drives Cassie and me to the dojo, which we have to ourselves. Cassie heads for the play-store; she brought Rover along so she could sell him stuff.

Bare feet, bow to the old guy, then Docker shows me how to do the ready stance, make a fist, and snap out a punch. Front stance, stepping punch, and downward block come next, all of which have fancy Japanese names and all of which have to be done just so. Then he shows me the rising block. My brain's on overload, I'll never dare use any of this against Floyd, and every time Docker touches me—adjusting my arm, my fist, or my posture—all I want to do is run for the door. Which I might be able to do marginally faster than last week.

At the end of the session, he says, "We'll meet again on Monday. Practice, Brick, that's the key. Every day if you can.

I'll loan you a book with photos of everything we've done so far. And I want you to read up on the philosophy behind karate." He looks me right in the eye. "Self-defense. Respect your opponent."

I'd agree to anything right now.

After we bow our way out the door, he gives me the book and drops us off at the end of his driveway. As we walk home, I say to Cassie, "Going to Docker's gym, that's our secret. If Floyd finds out, you won't be able to play with the store again."

"Rover paid $100 for Cheerios."

I hide the book and the weights in my closet, cook supper for me and Cassie, and we eat at the dining-room table. Floyd doesn't come home until I'm loading the dishwasher. He goes into the living room and turns on the TV. Ultimate Fighting.

FRIDAY, FLOYD leaves for work early, which means I can run before it gets too warm. I don't want him to know I've taken up running. The less he knows about me, the better.

Although Docker and I didn't seem to do much at the dojo, muscles I didn't know I owned are letting me know I do own them. Cassie's having a hissy fit as I lace my old sneakers.

"I want to go to Marigold's to play with Caramel."

"You can't."

"Why not?"

"Because." Because Tully thinks I'm pond scum. "I'm going for my run, then after breakfast we'll drive to the library. Or the beach. You like the beach."

"Can we take Caramel to the beach?"

"We'll go shopping later on. I'll buy you a present."

Opal has already left money in the jar for new sneakers, even though I leaned on her about Floyd and about babysitting as well. I'll never figure her out.

The whine escalates. "Caramel! I want Caramel."

"Shut up, Cassie! Opal's upstairs if you need anything and I'll be back in half an hour."

I slam the door on the way out, wondering what it would be like to have normal parents who look after their kids. Or to be an only child like Glenn.

For a change, I cross the bridge, walking fast up the hill, then jogging on the level. The air is cool, dew on the grass, birds yakking in the trees. For the space of three or four minutes, I jog along real easy, my pace smooth, arms pumping, back straight. Takes me by surprise.

I slow to a walk, doing some bicep curls. If I'm in shape at the start of hockey season, I might not hate it so much.

Jog some more, not as smooth this time. Hockey is Floyd's idea. The National Sport. More pressure is how I see it. At games, the crowd screaming when someone slams you into the boards, Floyd tight-faced if I don't slam back, yet furious if I get a penalty. I'm no bully on the ice because there's guys on the other teams a lot heavier than me. It'll be worse next season because I'll be on the bottom rung of Midget.

Floyd wants an enforcer for a son, another Brashear or Carcillo. The blood vessels in his forehead throbbed like they were going to burst when he found out Rebecca Sanger and Tiffany Gottrich were on our team.

In Novice and Atom, hockey was okay. We spent most of our time tripping over each other and shooting the puck to the opposing team; goals were scored because the net happened to get in the way. But in Peewee the coach and the parents, including Floyd, decided we were old enough to produce. On the drive to the rink, Floyd would outline what he expected of me. On the drive home, he'd conduct a detailed postmortem of all my failings.

No more high-fives on Beaver Lake.

My watch tells me I've been gone twenty-three minutes. I start back, jogging faster, pushing myself. It'd be neat to have one of those fancy belts that carry little flasks of water.

Sweat stings my eyes. Forgot my bandanna. Cassie's fault. My fifteenth birthday is in December. One year later, I'll shake the dust of Hilchey River Road off my sneakers forever.

In the meantime, I've worked out a strategy for school: keep my marks up until I graduate from grade nine, then pull out all the stops for the first term of grade ten. Can't hurt to have a brilliant report card for the high school in Halifax.

What will it be like to leave Cassie behind? My footsteps falter. I'll miss her. After all, she's my kid sister. She'll miss me too, I know she will, because I've been part of the furniture ever since she was born. She won't have to worry about her big brother getting it in the neck from Floyd, though; with me gone, his mood will vary between Relatively Neutral to Johnny Cash. That's a big plus. She'll be in school by the time I leave, and at Happy Whale Daycare after school—another plus.

Summers are the problem. I'll need a fulltime job in Halifax for July and August, so she won't be able to stay with me except on weekends. Maybe I could ask Rolf and Marigold to invite her to their place a couple of times a week in July and August.

She can be a real pain sometimes. But still.

6.1 ["Father and Son"]

AFTER A slow-jog down the hill and across the bridge, I take the driveway at a walk, enjoying the shade of the trees, blood thwacking my eardrums.

In the kitchen, I swig cold water straight from the tap.

Cassie's not downstairs. She wasn't outside, either. I stretch my quads and calves. "Cassie? Where are you?"

Probably in her room, sulking. I'll check on her, then do the weights. Wonder how long before I can actually feel a bicep?

She's not in her room. Opal and Floyd's bedroom door is shut, ladylike snores coming from the other side. The office is empty. Ditto the bathroom and my room. I take the stairs fast, search the main floor again, then the backyard, calling her name.

Caramel. She's gone to see Caramel.

I race down the driveway. We have an unbreakable rule—never leave the property without me.

A logging truck is coming down the hill, jake brakes like muffled gunshots.

I burst out of the end of the driveway, looking both ways. In the middle of the road, Caramel is lolloping toward me from Rolf's place, his pink tongue flopping. Cassie's running after him, her cheeks bright red. Behind me, the truck tires hit the slats on the bridge, that hollow echo of wood over water.

I yell, "Cassie, get off the road!"

Toes digging into the dirt, I run as I've never run before. Caramel sees me coming, heads right for me. Before he can dodge, I scoop him up under one arm. Cassie stops dead, squishing her eyes shut.

A horn blasts.

With my free hand I lift Cassie and vault toward the ditch. Her arms fasten around my neck, her chin banging my collarbone. The truck swerves and it's past us, throwing up stones, wind blowing my hair, grit in my eyes.

Rusty blue undercarriage. No logs.

If the truck had been loaded, could it have swerved?

I stand still on the shoulder of the road, head bowed, trying to breathe past the lock in my throat. Caramel licks my arm, squirming. Cassie's a dead weight. Slowly her hands loosen their grip. The sun strikes hot on the back of my neck.

I put her down. She's spilled juice on the front of her T-shirt. Grape juice. She's not supposed to pour her own.

Towering over her, wanting to shake her until her teeth bang together, I heave in another lungful of air, dust and all. My voice erupts, harsh, ugly. "That's the dumbest thing you ever did!"

She jams her thumb in her mouth. Her curls are stuck to her forehead.

"You nearly got us all killed! Chasing that fool dog down the middle of the road—what are you, a total idiot?"

Caramel is wriggling frantically under my arm. Cassie looks petrified.

I'd whack her if I wasn't holding the dog.

I say tightly, "We better take Caramel back to Marigold's."

I set a mean pace down the road, pulling her along with me. The puppy whines. "Shut up," I say, and he does.

Marigold's side door is open. I knock. From inside, Marigold calls, "I'll be right there."

I don't put Caramel down until the door's closed behind us. He stumbles to his bowl and slurps some water, then collapses in a heap on the floor. Marigold comes into the kitchen, a hair dryer in one hand.

I say in the same hard voice, "Cassie, tell Marigold what you did."

"I let Caramel out. I couldn't catch him. Brick's mad at me."

Not a tear in sight.

Awkwardly, Marigold stoops to Cassie's level. "You opened the side door?"

Cassie nods. "I'm sorry," she whispers.

"Did you knock first?" Another nod. "I was in the shower, and

Tully's sleeping in." Marigold pauses. "Did I just hear a logging truck?"

"No," I say.

"Brick saved us," Cassie says. "Me and Caramel."

Shut your trap.

Marigold says, "I think we all need a drink of juice. It looks like Caramel's worn out—where did he run?"

"Up the road and down." Cassie's chin quivers. "I tried to catch him. I ran and ran."

"Of course you did. I think you've learned your lesson, Cassie. Apple juice or cranberry?"

So we're sitting there drinking juice like it's a regular day, except none of us are saying much, when Tully wanders into the room, yawning. Shorts, bare feet, red hair tousled. She sees me and stops by the doorway. "What's up?"

Marigold says, "Would you take Cassie outside for a minute, Tully?"

Tully's eyes dart from me to Cassie. "Sure," she says.

Once she and Cassie have gone, Marigold says, "Tell me what happened with the truck."

"Nothing."

"Brick," she says, "we're going to sit here until you tell me."

Staring at my sneakers, I describe how Caramel and Cassie were running along the middle of the road and how we all scrambled for the ditch.

"Why was Cassie on the road by herself?" Marigold asks.

"I was out jogging. Opal must've slept in."

"I see."

Obviously Marigold doesn't think the mother of a four-year-old should sleep in. It's on the tip of my tongue to say, *Opal's not the problem at our house.*

"By the sound of it, you saved Cassie's life," Marigold says. "And Caramel's."

Heat creeps up my neck.

"I've complained about the logging trucks, how fast they drive after they cross the bridge." She reaches over, pats my knee. "You can bring Cassie here anytime, Brick."

The heat's reached my forehead. I gulp down the last of the juice. It's only 8:20. Feels like it should be suppertime. Before I lose my nerve, I ask, "Could I bring her next Monday afternoon about four thirty? Just until six."

"That's fine."

"You won't tell anyone about today?"

"I tell Rolf everything."

Oh man. "And Tully?"

"No, I won't tell Tully. And Rolf is closemouthed."

When I go outside to collect Cassie, she flinches away from me, just as if I did whack her. Tully gives me a dirty look. "What's up with Cassie? She won't say a word."

"Come on, Cassie, we're going home."

"I asked you a question!"

"I don't have to answer your stupid questions!"

"I'll ask my mom."

"Go right ahead."

I grip Cassie by the wrist and yank her across the lawn. Tully goes inside, slamming the door. As soon as we reach the road, I drop Cassie's arm.

One thing for sure. She won't run away again.

A vehicle is approaching behind us. I keep walking. The last person I want to see is Rolf.

The Hummer draws up alongside and Floyd says, "What were you doing at Rolf Langille's place?"

"They have a new puppy."

"We don't fraternize with the neighbors. Go home."

He accelerates, then turns into our driveway. If I'd stayed in bed this morning, none of this would have happened. Now Floyd's all geared up to go just when my face is almost back to normal, the last bruise a yellow blur on my jaw.

Once, I looked up the lyrics to "Father and Son," one of Floyd's top Johnny Cash songs, the whole point being that some things never change.

We trail down the driveway to the house. Cassie twists the doorknob and we walk inside. "Straight upstairs," I say.

The fear in her eyes—it'll be way better for her when I'm gone.

Floyd's waiting for me in the kitchen. Cassie skedaddles up the stairs.

"Good thing I forgot my laptop this morning, kiddo," he says. "I've told you before, we keep ourselves separate from the neighbors. I thought you had a brain under all that hair. Obedience isn't a difficult concept."

"Sorry."

"It's just as well your grandfather died before you were born. It saved him a lot of disappointment."

He does his hair-tugging, face-slapping gig, followed by one hard punch to the solar plexus. I go down, gasping for air. Face wet and it ain't sweat.

No front stance. No blocks. I'll call Docker later today, tell him I'm wasting his time and mine.

Floyd goes into his study, fetches his laptop, and he's gone. I contemplate staying where I am for the rest of the day. Would Opal even notice?

What's the solar plexus got to do with the sun? Why, out of the entire gene pool, was I picked to be Floyd's son?

Before she embraced the New Age, Opal used to drag me to church, where the pastor preached about suffering and how it ennobled the soul. Then there's Mr. Beamer, our social studies teacher, who's apt to make pronouncements. According to him, adversity builds character.

Mine should be a skyscraper by now.

But for five minutes this morning, I ran like I knew what I was doing. Like my body knew what it was doing.

AT THREE that afternoon, after I cut the grass as ordered by you-know-who, I'm standing in the shade of the pine trees near the woodpile, standing in front stance, trying to root my feet to the ground the way Docker said.

Doesn't take long to realize my thigh muscles are stronger than they were a week ago.

I've filled Cassie's plastic pool, so she's splashing away nearby, her back to me as she croons a mishmash of Dr. Seuss phrases to her inflatable frog. When I warned her not to tell anyone what I'm doing in the backyard, she just nodded. She hasn't spoken to me since this morning.

She won't forgive me until she's good and ready, I know that from experience.

I try the stepping punch, every now and then consulting the book Docker loaned me to see if I'm doing it right. To make a fist you have to fold your fingers and thumb a certain way, start the punch palm up, and switch at the last minute. Gives you power, that's what Docker said. I work on feeling that power. Helps me forget my sore chest.

The downward block, *gedan barai*, isn't too difficult. With all the blocks, you twist at the hip so you're less of a target. I like that idea.

The rising block, *age-uke*, is harder. Fists, arms, chest, hips, knees, and feet, they're all involved and you want them to work together, smooth and fast. Because I'm curious, I try *soto-uke*, the outside block, which protects your stomach instead of your head. For stomach, read *solar plexus*.

Sitting under the trees, I read the first chapter of the book. The name of the old guy in the photo at the dojo is Gichin Funakoshi; he founded Shotokan karate, the kind Docker teaches.

Summer is interminable. Is that why I'm doing this?

At seven thirty, Cassie's bedtime, she cleans her teeth, darts across the hall, and shuts the door in my face.

6.2 [nothing succeeds like success]

EVEN THOUGH Floyd did his thing yesterday, which means he should leave me alone the next couple of weeks, AQ is sky-high when I wake up the next morning. What's going on?

He's on Saturday shift again, so I don't get up until he's gone. Cassie's still in her room. No, it did not hurt my feelings that she wouldn't let me kiss her good night. I pull on my sweats and head outdoors.

Time for a new graph.

```
Horizontal axis: endorphins
Vertical axis:   AQ
Result:          a 45° downward slope. Down is good.
```

As I reach the end of the driveway, Glenn is walking across the bridge away from our place, Igor on his long blue leash. Everything I normally keep tamped down and under control erupts to the surface. Graphs and downward slopes, what use are they? Action is what I need.

I jog toward them. When Glenn catches sight of me, he winds the leash around his left wrist and positions his feet in a piss-poor imitation of front stance. Igor skitters away, tail curled between his legs, until the leash goes taut.

"You're a real jerk, Glenn," I say. "You don't even have the sense to run—and you're supposed to be smart. Don't you understand you're just begging for it?"

"If I'm a jerk, at least I'm a jerk with friends," Glenn says and jabs with his free fist.

But somehow my left arm blocks his and the jab hits air. I aim a stepping punch at his chest. He ducks, so it skids off his shoulder. Grunting, he tries to punch me again. No trouble to get his arm behind his back, pull up on it, and keep pulling.

His face convulses. Although he's gritting his teeth, the groans are escaping anyway. I could let go. I don't. Instead, I keep lifting until his toes are barely touching the ground, more and more of his weight on his shoulder.

What if I dislocate it? X-ray, surgery, rehab, who gives a shit.

Five seconds, six seconds, seven seconds ... a tear hangs on Glenn's lashes, drips to his cheek, trickles down it. Another one follows, making a small wet patch on his T-shirt.

I'm staring at him. I've done it. I've made Glenn Semple cry.

I let go. He staggers into the metal railing of the bridge,

hunched over, eyes squeezed shut. I want to say something, but I don't know what to say.

Wiping my hands down the side of my sweats, I hurry past Igor and start running up the hill, running as if six starving Dobermans are after me.

At first each step is a killer, rattling my ribcage where Floyd hit me. But if Docker can be persistent, so can I. My feet fly along the dirt road; they're not stopping for anyone because they're running away from themselves. They don't quit until my legs are quivering with strain, until my breath is tearing at my throat and a stitch rips my side.

Hunched over like Glenn, I drag air into my lungs. I always thought that if only I could make Glenn Semple cry, I'd feel better.

CASSIE IS sitting at the kitchen table munching dry Cheerios. She doesn't look up when I walk in. I don't give myself time to think.

"Cassie, I shouldn't have yelled at you yesterday. Even though you scared me half to death."

She picks up a Cheerio, rolls it along the tablecloth until it drops off the edge to the floor. Then she picks up another one.

"It's as though Floyd took over," I say desperately. "Floyd inside me, his words coming out my mouth ... oh man, I'm losing it. It's like I didn't have a choice—I couldn't help it. I don't want to turn into Floyd. I hate him!"

I'm talking to myself now—even I know that. Maybe I am losing it. One slap too many to the side of the head.

"You were scary," she whispers. "Scary like him."

At least she's looking at me. "I won't act like Floyd again, Cassie, I swear I won't." Although how can I swear to anything if stuff spews out before I can put the brakes on?

"Okay," she says. "You gonna kiss me when I go to bed tonight?"

"If you want me to."

She nods. So I've fixed one thing, at least. Hold that thought.

I can't. I sit down next to her, elbows on the table, and dig my fingers into my scalp. This morning on the bridge, I blocked Glenn's punch. A rough-and-ready block, but still a block. Then I made a fist and tried to put power behind it. Doesn't matter that it missed the target.

If Docker finds out, he'll drop me quicker than a front kick.

Go ahead, Brick, say it. You used karate on Glenn like Floyd uses boxing on you.

6.3 [naked]

I DON'T know what I'm trying to fix when I spend a couple of hours on weights and karate after lunch. I go over—again and again—the front stance, stepping punch, and the three blocks. Flipping ahead in the book, I try the reverse punch, side stance, and side snap kick.

Side kicks are cool.

Docker wouldn't approve of me jumping around in the book. Docker isn't here.

Later, Cassie and I drive to town on the ATV. In case Snyder's around, I park beside Sobeys where there are more people. Then I take Cassie to the toy department at Zellers.

"You can buy anything you want, up to fifteen dollars," I say. "How about a nice white teddy bear? Aren't you tired of Rover?"

Her jaw juts. "I love Rover. I want to buy something for Caramel at the pet store."

No point arguing. After a lot of thought, she picks out a rawhide stick he'll probably barf on Marigold's clean floor, a rubber ball, and a ceramic dish with a picture of a puppy wearing a crown and a silly grin. Total, fourteen dollars and sixty-nine cents. Now all we have to do is deliver them.

Don't fraternize with the neighbors.

Cassie needs Caramel, Marigold, and Rolf. Perhaps she even needs Tully. We'll just have to be careful.

Once we're done at the pet store—after Cassie's talked to four kittens and a turtle shell, no turtle visible—we go to the sports store, where I find a pair of Nike look-alikes, half-price. Excellent support and cushioning, the sales guy says.

If I run fast enough, no one can read the label.

The barber is the next stop. Only two people ahead of me, one of them a guy in my grade who looks at Cassie, looks at me, and sneers.

MacAvoy, Brickson. Popularity 101: F.

Magazines, a coloring book, and some crayons are heaped on the table. Cassie chooses purple for the trees and orange for the people, and that keeps her quiet.

When it's my turn, I ask for a buzz cut. The barber wraps me in a black cape. Then he turns on his electric clippers and cuts a swath from forehead to nape, like he's mowing long grass. I want to change my mind. I want to close my eyes. I don't do either one. I've had enough of Floyd yanking me around by the hair. If he's going to slap me, he'll have to grab my ear.

Right, Brick, give him a new challenge. He'll switch from slaps to punches. I should have thought this through. The clippers buzz louder than a swarm of hornets.

Finally, with a flourish, the barber removes the cape from my shoulders. "Looks good on you," he says.

In the mirror I see a tall kid with gray eyes like Floyd's and a gaunt face. Cheekbones I never noticed before. Opal's cheekbones.

The Chinless Wonder ... actually, my chin's not so bad.

I look older. More exposed.

Tougher?

I wish.

"Thanks," I say, and pay the barber out of the change from the Nikes. From the look on his face, I realize he expects a tip. Flustered, I slap a toonie on the counter. There's still nearly thirteen dollars left for the stash.

Instead, wearing my new sneakers and a stubble of dark hair, I take Cassie to McDonald's. On the back of the place mat, they've printed the calories in a Big Mac. I'm skinny. Running burns calories. I order two plus a large fries for me, and chicken fingers with sweet-and-sour sauce for Cassie.

"Can we give Caramel his presents today?" she asks.

I'm in so deep, one more infraction won't count. "We'll park the ATV under the trees at Marigold's, so Floyd won't know we're there."

"Yep." She licks sauce from her fingers.

It'll be my fault if she turns into a champion liar.

6.4 [nakeder (I know, there's no such word)]

WE WALK out of McDonald's and there she is, smack-dab in front of me. Kendra Ryan from Happy Whale Daycare. Eight years since I've seen her. My jaw just about hits my toenails and my knees go weak.

"Brick?" she says. "Brick MacAvoy?" Same eyes like melted chocolate, same flyaway hair like she stuck her finger in a light socket.

"Hi," I say.

She throws her arms around me. "I'm so glad to see you! I left a message with your father last night, but he must have forgotten to give it to you."

I stand like a stick. The phone rang about eight thirty last night. He didn't forget.

"Gary and I are staying in Halifax because he's here on business, so I decided to rent a car today. Our first trip with no kids—we have a girl, five, and a boy, three ... and who's this?"

Gary must be the husband. "Er ... my sister, Cassie."

Kendra kneels down, smiling at Cassie. "Do you know what? I started looking after your brother when he was six weeks old. Once he was big enough, I taught him how to push a broom around and wash dishes and bake cookies with Smarties on top. Do you like Smarties?"

"Gummi bears," Cassie says and smiles back. Kendra's like that. Hard to resist.

"Looks as if you were at the beach—you have sand between your toes."

"Brick builded me a castle."

"That's another thing we used to do." Kendra stands up and turns the smile on me. "I can't get over how tall you are! Have you got time for coffee?"

"We're on our way to visit a neighbor."

"I'll walk with you, then. Does your mother still work at Shoppers?"

"No. Floyd still sells cars, though, and we live in the same house."

She grimaces. "I had to drive you home a few times. Your house always made me feel claustrophobic—dark shingles, trees crammed against the windows. I was hoping you'd have moved by now ... So, how's life treating you, Brick? Tell me about yourself."

I walk faster. "Not much to tell."

But she's persistent like Docker. Age, grade, sports, and books take us to the ATV.

"Good to see you, Kendra," I say, shifting from foot to foot.

"I'm sorry I left the daycare so suddenly," she says. "I didn't even have the chance to say good-bye. Were you ever told what happened?"

"Mrs. Sanger said your mother was ill. Later, she told us she'd died." And every day for weeks after that, I confidently waited for Kendra to come back to Happy Whale.

"My mother had a stroke that put her in ICU, so I flew to Winnipeg on a Sunday morning. At the airport, when I called your place, your father said you were out playing. Same thing when I phoned the following week. I stayed out West until my mother died six months later—I'd met Gary by then. We moved to Toronto and I never came back here." She sighs. "Of all the kids, you were the one I missed the most."

I cried and cried when you left. Floyd called me a sissy and threatened to lock me in the cellar if I didn't stop. So I stopped.

"Oh," I say.

"You used to come to daycare after school, remember? Some days you'd just follow me around, as if you needed something but you didn't know how to ask or what to ask for ... I don't know if I gave it to you."

"You were good to me," I say. *You were my real mother ... If you give me another hug, I'll be bawling like that six-year-old.* "We gotta go."

She hesitates. "Things have turned out okay for you?"

"Yeah." What good would it do to tell the truth? She can't fix Floyd's clock when he's in Hilchey Bay and she's in Toronto.

Kendra takes a business card out of her wallet. "You can reach me by phone or e-mail. Let's keep in touch ... please."

"Sure. Sure we will."

"Bye, Cassie," she says. "Don't eat too many gummi bears." She rests her hand on my arm. "Take care, Brick. I don't know if you're ever likely to come to Toronto—but if you do, you could stay with us for as long as you want."

I swallow hard. "Thanks. Let's go, Cassie."

As I drive away, Kendra waves at us. Cassie waves back. As if it were yesterday, I can picture all us kids playing Simple Simon one winter day in the playground, Kendra yelling louder than the rest of us put together. My scarf had red and green stripes.

I wonder what happened to that scarf.

I PARK the ATV in the shade of the trees at Rolf's.

Floyd didn't even have the decency to tell his six-year-old son that Kendra had phoned to say good-bye. If I'd known, I wouldn't have felt so abandoned.

No way to untangle the hard knot of anger in my chest.

I say to Cassie, "We won't tell anyone about meeting Kendra, okay?"

She nods. "She's nice. Will you make me cookies with Smarties on top?"

"We'll see."

I knock on the door. Tully opens it. "You cut your hair!" she says, then blushes a fiery red.

Cassie says, waving the bag over the puppy's head, "Presents, Caramel!"

I don't say anything. Mostly I'm trying to keep my eyes off Tully's skimpy tank top. I didn't know she owned one.

Caramel's bowl goes on the kitchen floor, filled with water; he ignores it, shaking the strip of rawhide, drooling on the linoleum, and growling. Tully says, "He can chew on it for five minutes, Cassie, then we'll take him outdoors to play ball."

"Where's Marigold?" Cassie says.

"She's not home."

I feel like my collar's too tight. I'm wearing a T-shirt. It doesn't have a collar. "I'll wait on the step," I say, and escape. Behind the fire pit on the back lawn, Rolf has rigged a plastic line the width of their lot, with a rope dangling from it on a swivel. Marigold must have told him how Caramel ran away.

When Tully and Cassie come outside, Caramel on his leash, I say, "Cassie, you'll have to play behind the house."

"Why?" Tully asks.

Cassie pokes at the grass. I say, "I'm not supposed to bring her here."

"Aren't we good enough for you?"

She's pulled a shirt over her tank top. Her hair's so bright a guy could scald his hands. "Floyd doesn't like us associating with the neighbors."

"So he's a snob. Big deal."

"Tully, just do it, okay?"

With real curiosity, she says, "Do you always obey your father? Haven't you heard about teenage rebellion?"

"I'm too busy looking after Cassie to have time to rebel. And I don't see *you* kicking off the traces."

The curiosity is still there, though, along with something else that's harder to read.

She crouches beside Cassie. "Do you want to play behind the house?"

As Cassie gives me one of her looks, I can almost read Tully's mind. *Poor kid's so scared of Brick she won't open her mouth.* Fine by me. It feels a whole lot safer with Tully in hostility mode.

But when she turns to Cassie, she's all smiles. "How about I fix Caramel's line so he can't be seen from the road?"

Cassie skips into the backyard. "C'mon, Caramel."

Tully wedges several clothes pegs to the line to keep Caramel's rope behind the house, then attaches the puppy's collar to the rope. When she throws the new rubber ball, Caramel and Cassie chase after it. Caramel wins. Sitting on the ATV, I run my hands over the bristles on my scalp, take out Docker's book, and study the photos, listening to Cassie and Tully laugh. I'm used to being on my own. Why would I want to join them?

Can't bring myself to practice any blocks and kicks. Tully would think I'm working on *Bullying for Dummies*.

FLOYD AND Opal are out when we arrive home. I deal with supper, dishes, TV, Cassie's bath, three picture books, pleas for more, and a kiss good night, and finally I'm alone in my room.

Ever since we met Kendra, my chest has felt clogged. It's not ordinary, everyday anger. It's rage. I contemplate going downstairs, taking Floyd's Eric Lindros mug out of the cupboard, and smashing it in the sink. I pick up the tennis book, put it down again. Floyd's right. I'm chinless, useless, gutless, hopeless.

Kendra did phone me. Twice. She tried again last night.

Of all the kids, you were the one I missed the most.

She missed me ... Kendra missed me. Every day after school, she used to give me a chocolate chip cookie on my special plate, which had blue dolphins leaping around the edge. It didn't matter to me that by Friday the cookies were getting stale.

She saved my life.

I sit down on the bed, listening to the maple leaves brush against the window. Happiness because Kendra cared enough to miss me, sadness because I lost her, gratitude that she found me again ... and underneath it all, rage that Floyd was so mean. So freaking, goddamn mean.

SUNDAY. FLOYD and Opal come downstairs at noon, her in a clinging, satin robe. I stare into the saucepan where I'm heating hot dogs for Cassie. The water's simmering, a film of grease on the surface.

Opal says blankly, "Your hair! You look like Thaddeus. Doesn't he, Floyd?"

Floyd's gone dead white, as though a ghost with a buzz cut is cooking the hot dogs.

"Be quiet, Opal."

"Thaddeus is six feet under," Opal says, "which is the best place for him as far as I'm concerned, I don't care if he was your father—and I wish you'd quit acting as though he could walk in the door any minute."

"I told you to be quiet!"

"It's funny," she says, head to one side as she gazes at me, "I never realized how much you take after your grandfather, Brick."

"He always looked like my father," Floyd says.

"Is that why you hit me?" I blurt.

Two strides and he's snapped his hand around my wrist like a manacle. "I discipline you to make something of you—you're a poor excuse for a son."

My fingers tighten around the handle. What would happen if I let fly with it, hot dogs in his hair, grease sliding down his cheeks?

As if he can read my mind, Floyd says softly, "Don't get too smart. Haircut or not, I can still slap you around."

"Yeah, right."

"And don't get lippy." He tugs me closer. He needs a shave. "Where did you get the money to pay the barber?"

"Opal gave me money for sneakers. They were on sale."

"Give her the change. All of it. From now on, you'll account for every penny you spend."

I'm sick of his games. His sick games.

Opal says edgily, "It's Sunday, Floyd. Give it a rest."

He lets go of my arm and twists my earlobe. "Don't you forget who's boss."

Him and Thaddeus. Two for the price of one.

7.1 [42 km/hr]

LIKE A man obsessed, Floyd works all Sunday afternoon and into the evening on one of the new jigsaws (van Gogh's *Pink Peach Trees*); this puts him in a good mood. Still, the Hummer starting up on Monday morning is the best sound in the world. I'm actually looking forward to my run. Opal's home, so I don't have to worry about Cassie.

In the living room, the peach trees are already dismantled, and another box is sitting on the card table. Monet's *Waterlilies*. I wouldn't mind working on that myself. Weird.

I start out slow, crossing the bridge, taking the hill at a jog. I feel lighter without all that hair. On the level I speed up, breathing easy, landing on the balls of my feet, arms and ankles loose. Toe, heel, toe, heel, smooth strides that gobble up the distance. For the first time in my life, I've found something that fits.

Although our school doesn't do much in the way of track and field, when I move to Halifax they'll have proper coaches and teams. In the meantime, the library would have books on running.

Is it speed I'm after? Or endurance? The endurance to keep running and running and running ... just me and the dirt under my feet.

A logging truck roars down the road, churning up dust. I narrow my eyes to slits, breathe shallow, and slow to a walk. Will I ever forget Cassie's face, scrunched up in terror?

When I turn around to run home, the breeze is cool on my face. Daisies sway in the ditch. A hawk soars overhead, light shining through its tail feathers, deep orange. Three crows dive-bomb it, squawking up a storm. Seems like I never noticed these things before.

Running down a hill is almost as hard as running up it. My new nearly-Nikes thud across the bridge. Didn't even have to break them in.

Something's running toward me, running faster than I thought anything could run. With a shock of recognition, I see it's Igor, body compact, paws skimming the ground, the pale blue leash whipping behind him. He's back on the race track, you don't have to be a genius to see that.

One logging truck and he's a goner.

Glenn nowhere to be seen.

I skid to a halt. He's nearly up to me; I'm not sure he even sees me. Didn't I read somewhere that a greyhound will run until his heart gives out?

At the last minute I lunge for him. He swerves and snaps at

me, breaking stride, slowing fractionally. I stamp both feet on the leash, watch it slide under my sneakers, grinding through the dirt. Grab for it with my bare hands.

The edges score my palm. Frantically I make a fist. Then the loop catches on my thumb and somehow I thrust my other hand through it.

The jolt pulls me to my knees. For a couple of seconds I'm dragged along by a speed-crazed greyhound, gravel ripping my sweats. I yelp. Igor tumbles in a heap on the bridge.

Sides heaving, jaws agape, he raises his head and looks right at me. Through me, beyond me, his gaze still on the track, blind to anything but distance.

A bird calls from the maples; another one answers across the road. Very slowly, the dog comes back to himself, his eyes now filled with a sadness so intense that I say softly, "It's okay, Igor, it's okay ... I'll take you home."

He starts to tremble. Because he's exhausted? Or because he recognizes my voice?

Three days past my eighth birthday, a stray dog turns up at our place. No collar, nothing much to look at, hips caved in. I steal some leftover spaghetti from the refrigerator, spooning it into a bowl that I hide in the bushes in back of the garage, and fill another bowl with water. Next day I bring him canned stew mixed with bread.

I name him Wilbur. By the fourth day, although he still won't let me touch him, he doesn't run away when he sees me coming. He waits a minute or two, tail between his legs, then buries his nose in the bowl, sucking up the food in noisy gulps. I tell him things I can't tell anyone else.

The fifth day is Saturday. I feed him early, before Floyd and Opal are up. After lunch, I go down to the river with my fleet of plastic boats, hoping he'll join me. There's a shallow pool where I often wade, the water dark brown with blobs of foam from the current. The boats are drifting in lazy circles around the pool when I hear two shots, one right after the other. They echo through the trees. Then there's only the sound of the river.

The shots have come from our place.

One of my boats escapes from the pool. Caught by the current, it whirls in the eddies, tips over, bashes nose-first into a rock. Smashing at the water with my fists, I shove all the boats into the current, watching them lurch and toss and go under.

When I go home, there's a patch of freshly turned dirt behind the garage.

7.2 [first aid]

WINCING, MAKING sure I have a good grip on the leash, I get to my feet. We walk down the road, Igor's head hanging. His coat, which is a splotchy mix of black, brown, and gray, is slick with sweat. I go faster, ignoring the pain in my knees; he trots along behind me, the leash slack.

I'll never be able to throw rocks at him again.

At the end of the road, the Semples' battered old Volkswagen is backing out of their driveway. Mr. Semple sees us right away, parks partly on the road, and clambers out. Glenn leaps out the other side. They both hurry toward us. As Glenn falls on his knees beside Igor, the dog buries his nose in Glenn's armpit.

Mr. Semple is shorter than me. He's wearing blue corduroy shorts that Floyd wouldn't be caught dead in. His spectacles are round with gold frames, and a rim of curly gray hair circles his head.

I pass him the leash. "I stopped Igor near the bridge."

"He got away from Glenn at MacTaggart's Store. Glenn just returned home, so we were starting out to look for him. I don't think I know you—do you live around here?"

Glenn hasn't told him about me? "Brick MacAvoy. I live up the road."

"Of course—Floyd's son." He holds out his hand to shake mine, which is when we both realize my palm is bleeding.

He says, "Come inside and we'll clean that up. How did you manage to catch Igor?"

"I have to—"

"No, no, my boy, no arguments. Bring Igor inside, Glenn, and give him a drink."

My eyes dart up and down the road. No sign of the Hummer.

Their house, painted dark green, is surrounded by neatly mowed grass. A hammock hangs between two apple trees.

In the kitchen, copper saucepans dangle from the ceiling among bunches of herbs. Pots of scarlet geraniums sit on the windowsills. There are books on the pine shelves, the counter, the table, the floor, and the chairs—enough books to make me hyperventilate.

In one corner, a metal stand holds a flute and some sheet music. Music is being piped from the stereo into the kitchen, wild, energetic music that's a long way from hard rock.

Mr. Semple pulls out a chair for me and bustles off to the bathroom. Once Glenn has unclipped Igor's leash and topped up his water bowl, the dog heads right for it. Glenn says, staring at Igor, "Thanks for stopping him. I don't ... well, thanks."

No need to answer because Mr. Semple comes back in. He fills a basin with warm water and dumps in some disinfectant that turns it cloudy. "Sorry, but this will hurt," he says, taking my hands and lowering them into the water.

Breath whistles through my teeth. "We don't want the cuts to get infected," he says as he takes the cap off a tube of antibiotic cream. "Glenn, why don't you pour Brick some juice? Pomegranate or apricot, Brick?"

"Uh ... apricot."

Mr. Semple blots my hands dry, picks out bits of dirt with tweezers, then dabs the cuts with cream; although his fingers are pudgy, they're deft and gentle. Last, he puts Band-Aids on the cuts. "That should do it. But keep an eye on them. And, Brick, thank you so much for bringing Igor home. Glenn, have you thanked him?"

"I already did."

"You don't sound terribly grateful."

"I am. I really am." His arm looped around Igor's shoulders, Glenn adds, "I didn't think you liked dogs, Brick. Especially Igor."

"Guess I changed my mind."

The stereo's changed to a violin winding a melody around the occasional soft notes of a piano. It's the saddest music I ever heard.

"What's that called? That music."

"Ravel's 'Kaddish,'" Mr. Semple says.

I must look blank as an empty page. "Ravel was a French composer who died in 1937," he says. "*Kaddish* is the Jewish prayer for the dead."

"It sounds like stones dropping into water."

"Hmm ... interesting analogy."

"I listen to AC/DC," I say, Mr. Tough Guy.

"*For Those About to Rock* tops my chart," says Mr. Semple, and suddenly the two of us are laughing.

Glenn says to me, "I never heard you laugh before."

"It's not like we hang out together."

"Why did you cut your hair?"

"Cooler. For summer." I gulp down the apricot juice, which tastes great, and say no to a homemade gingersnap even though I'm hungry enough to devour the whole can. "I gotta go. Cassie'll be wanting her breakfast—she's my little sister."

Mr. Semple's eyes sharpen behind his glasses. "Isn't your mother home?"

"She's home. But she might still be asleep."

When I stand up, Mr. Semple says, "Your knees! Here, we'd better—"

"I really have to go." Sunlight glints on the copper saucepans; one of the books sitting on the table is about Tibet. "I'll clean them up later."

"Be sure you do. But at least let me drive you home."

The VW is still parked partway into the road. Mr. Semple gives it too much accelerator when he reverses and the tires spin in the dirt. Grinding the gears as he goes into first, he says, "I can't tell you how grateful we are. Glenn thinks the world of that dog. He would have been devastated if anything had happened to him, particularly since he's the one who was responsible for the dog getting loose. He was trying to open a chocolate bar when a cat ran past." He skips second gear altogether, straight to third. The revs drop alarmingly. "Are you a reader?"

"Yeah, I like to read."

"One never knows these days. The next time you're in town, I want you to drop into the store. You can pick out any book you'd like, on the house. A small token of our appreciation—mine and Glenn's."

I flush scarlet. *A tear trickling down Glenn's cheek, Igor shivering at the end of his leash ...*

7.3 [interest is mounting daily]

AS WE drive past, Della Barnes is in her front garden cutting the grass, pushing the power mower up the slope with grim purpose. A germ of an idea takes hold.

"You can let me out here, Mr. Semple. Thanks for the drive."

"You're welcome. Don't forget about the book."

I watch him turn around with another clash of gears; it's a wonder the VW still has a clutch. Then I walk back down the road and stand there until Della turns the mower off. The silence feels loud.

"I'll cut your grass for you," I say. "For the rest of the summer. If you want."

She's skinny like me, wearing baggy trousers and a man's shirt, her face weathered and wrinkly, her hair in a loose knot that droops over one ear. "How much?"

I make a wild guess. "Twenty bucks. Can I bring my little sister? She's good—she wouldn't be in the way."

"We haven't allowed children on the property since last summer, when three boys from Swamp Road tore every rose off the bushes."

"I'd have to check whether she could stay with Marigold Langille ... I can only work weekdays, between eight and five."

"It's usually the employer who lays down the terms."

The stash. Remember the stash. "Rolf Langille, he'll give you a reference."

"I don't even know your name."

"Brick MacAvoy. From across the road."

"Ah. You'd better see how much grass there is before you decide."

Ah? What does that mean? I walk across the strip of mown grass between flowers as bright as Cassie's crayons; but it's the scent that wallops me. Roses, lilies, a vine with little red trumpets, spikes of blue flowers with silver leaves—they all perfume the air and I'm starting to sound like those poets we slogged through last term. Wordsworth. Keats. Dickinson.

The back has a vegetable garden with a high fence to keep deer out, a deck with more vines, a tumbledown rock wall, and more flowerbeds. Also more lawn. A lot more lawn, sloping to the trees and the river.

Della says, "You have to mow the grass, then clip around the trees and flowerbeds. I use old-fashioned shears because it's too easy to do damage with a weed eater. In summer it needs cutting at least once a week. Thirty dollars. Can you start today?"

I blink. "I'll have to ask Marigold first."

"I'll leave the mower behind the house. Gas in the shed, clippers hanging on the wall." She gives a brisk nod. "I'd much rather garden than mow. Rolf's a good man. If he approves of you, I'm willing to give you a try."

I walk home, my head reeling. A free book—assuming I've got the nerve to pick it up—and a job.

Total number of dogs saved in four days: two.

AN HOUR later, I've changed out of my torn sweats, dropped Cassie off at Marigold's, and I'm on my way to Della's. I'm not just fraternizing with the neighbors, I'm practically moving in with them.

When I go around back to get the mower, Della's spraying the rose bushes. Her sister is sitting on the deck in the shade. Opal told me that she's blind.

Della says, "Agnes, this is Brick MacAvoy."

"Hi," I say.

Agnes looks right at me. Spooky. She says calmly, "Hello, Brick."

My synapses earn their keep. The smelly flowers—they're for Agnes. I smile at Della, a smile I really mean, and she smiles back.

She's never once smiled at me at the post office.

To protect my hands, I'm wearing my work gloves. Nothing I can do about my knees. Determined to do the best job I can, I push the mower to the front yard and yank on the cord.

TWO HOURS later, Della inspects what I've done. She makes me clip around the herb garden again, but that's all. "Excellent," she says. "I'll get your money."

She gives me three crisp, new ten-dollar bills. "Phone me or drop by in four or five days, and we'll set the date for the next mowing," she says. "Thank you, Brick."

"You're welcome," I say, suave as Mr. Semple.

At four o'clock I take the ATV to town, deposit my thirty dollars in the bank, and go to the dojo for my second lesson.

How many times today have I broken The Law According to Floyd?

8.1 [*kiai*]

DOCKER'S WAITING for me. "Neat haircut," he says. "We'll warm up and go through last week's moves."

Soon as I make a fist, he's onto me, unfolding my palm. "What's this? A for-real ATV accident?"

"Fell. Running."

"You don't have to lie to me, Brick. Anything said in this room stays here."

For once, I was telling the truth. Although not the whole truth. Talking fast, I tell him how I caught Igor.

"Good for you," he says, then fetches two elasticized bandages that he slips over the Band-Aids on my hands.

"Front stance," he says, all business. "*Zenkutsu-dachi.*"

After we go over the downward block and the rising block, he shows me the outside block that I've been practicing on my own. I catch on fast. He's pleased, I can tell.

Next is the back stance, which is tricky, and the knife-hand block, *shuto-uke*. I like *shuto-uke* because it's another block that protects the solar plexus. By the time we're done, I'm sweating. He's not finished, though.

"We'll do a series of stepping punches," he says. "*Kiai* on the third punch."

Kiai is a loud martial shout that helps with breathing, scares the heck out of your opponents, and focuses power. The first time, a feeble croak comes out of my mouth. Three more punches, and I try again. Another sick-crow sound. Once more, same result.

I keep trying. I do. But there's a band around my throat and AQ's hitting the roof. Docker says quietly, "It wouldn't hurt to let it all out."

Anxiety flips into rage—I want to hit him so bad I can taste it. He says, unsmiling, "Lotta anger in you. This might be the safest place for you to get rid of it. Go ahead, Brick. I can look after myself."

But the moment has passed. "I can't stay much longer," I mumble. "I have to pick Cassie up at Rolf's."

"Try *kiai* at home," he says, as if nothing happened. "You're doing fine—making real progress."

We stretch and bow, and I give him back the bandages. On the way out the door, he passes me a slip of paper. "Memorize these by Thursday. I call them the five principles of the dojo."

Seek perfection of character

Be faithful

Endeavour

Respect others

Refrain from violent behavior

Like, I should just pass the paper to Floyd.

8.2 [*kumite* (sparring)]

CARAMEL GREETS me as if I'm his best buddy, his rump wriggling, his nose butting my ankles. As I bend over to pat him, tears suddenly blur my vision.

It's Docker's fault, him and his frigging *kiai*. Emotions are best kept six feet under, the same place they put Thaddeus—I learned *that* the first time Floyd hit me. I turn my back and pat Caramel some more, blinking like crazy.

If I hadn't been feeding Wilbur, encouraging him to hang around our place, he might still be alive.

When I finally stand up, Cassie's tucking into a salad as though she eats lettuce every day of the week, Rover propped on a stool next to her. Marigold fills my plate and Tully, as usual, ignores me. Rolf's eyes flick to my haircut; he rubs the bald spot on his scalp and winks at me.

Hoping I sound halfway normal, I say, "I'm mowing the grass for Della Barnes, Rolf—told her you'd give her a reference if she wants one."

"I was planning on cutting her grass," Tully snaps, "now that I'm not babysitting the Zwicker twins."

I scowl at her. "How was I to know?"

She scowls back. I shovel in some tuna casserole, which has crumbs and grated cheese baked crisp on the top.

Another thing that helps AQ is eating.

By the time the meal's over, I could put my head down on the table and fall asleep. "Thanks a lot, Marigold—it's great I don't have to go home and cook supper."

"Doesn't your mother feed you?" Tully says rudely.

"She's works. So she's out a lot."

Rolf drawls, "You two scrap like stray cats."

It doesn't seem to bother him. Amazing.

Before I climb on the ATV, I say to Cassie, "If Floyd asks, we ate at McDonald's."

"Chicken fingers," Cassie says.

"Right. Chicken fingers."

He doesn't ask because his full attention is on the Monet puzzle, his hand hovering over the array of pieces that make up the pale turquoise water. I stop, gazing down at them. They're all funny shapes.

"The lilies were easy," Floyd says. "But the rest is a real challenge."

A piece jumps out at me. "Can I?"

"Fill your boots."

So I pick up the piece and bingo, it fits neat as can be into two adjoining pieces.

"Good job," Floyd says, as casually as if he says this to me every day of the week.

You want to know how this makes me feel? Like the hawk sailing toward the sun. Like I want to lay my head down on the water lilies and weep.

I can't come up with even a smidgen of anger.

I walk upstairs to the bathroom and gaze in the mirror. Who is this guy who looks like a Wanted poster at the RCMP detachment? Or like the passport photo of someone who doesn't know where he's going and wishes he gave a damn?

Before I go to bed, I force myself to read chapter five about bullying.

8.3 [white knight II]

NEXT MORNING all I'm good for is a combination of walking and jogging. I take #539 and Swamp Road for a change. It's not exactly raining—somewhere between mist and drizzle. Good thing I got to Della before Tully; if I cut the grass six or seven times, that's another $200 in my savings account.

I wonder who else would give me a job. Too risky to put a sign up at MacTaggart's.

I'm thirsty, so I stop in there, where I'm charged two bucks for a measly bottle of water. I glug it down and head outside.

Samson Donovan is zigzagging across the parking lot, kicking a stone with the toe of his sneaker. I lift him off the ground, turn him upside down, shake him, and watch coins rain out of his pockets.

Pennies and nickels. No dimes.

No quarters, either.

I lower him to the ground, right side up, and hear myself say, "I shouldn't have done that."

He's standing exactly where I put him, jacket rucked around his shoulders; it's not hard to see he had strawberry jam for breakfast. Kneeling, I start gathering the coins, passing him half a dozen. His fingernails are dirty.

When I've given him the last penny, I stand up. "I won't hassle you anymore. You or your brother."

Then I take off down the road, running along the shoulder as though the cops are after me. Likely he's been saving that money for candy. Gummi bears ... whatever.

At the turnoff to River Road, I slow to a walk. What kind of a creep am I? Lorne, white-faced, bug-eyed whenever he sees me coming. Gary Sanger, crying as he passes over his lunch money. Lucas, flat on the floor on top of his caramel chunk cookies.

If I quit bullying, AQ will be out of control. If Floyd would leave me alone, I wouldn't need to bully.

Floyd leaving me alone? Dream on. Who else would he pick on if he didn't have me?

I'm so scared of him. So fricking scared.

NO TRUCK in the driveway at Rolf's place, and no sign of Marigold or Caramel. A ladder is leaning against the side of the garage. Crouched on the roof is a girl with bright red hair. Tully Langille, who's scared of heights, on top of the garage? Now, there's a golden opportunity.

The rule flashes through my head as though Docker's standing in front of me in his white *gi: Seek perfection of character.*

When you live with Floyd, high-minded principles are about as useful as skates on a dog. I shout, "You taking up hang gliding?"

Her head jerks around. "Go away."

Almost, I do. Almost. "What if I take the ladder away instead?"

"Don't you dare!"

"Why don't you explain what you're doing up there?"

"What does it look like?" If a voice can sound aggressive, mortified, and desperate all at the same time, hers does.

I walk closer. "Looks like you're glued to the shingles."

She says, talking fast, "Mom's gone to town with Rolf for a doctor's appointment. I saw a baby robin fall out of the nest onto the roof—it was trying to fly. So I got out the ladder. Climbed it without thinking what I was doing. The bird's still here, so the parents keep dive-bombing me. I'm scared it'll die. Not that you'd care."

"Gimme one good reason why I should."

"How would you like to fall out of the nest and no one rescue you?"

Story of my life.

Tully's head is bowed again. "It's suffering," she says, so low I can scarcely hear her.

Even I can see that she's the one who's suffering. If she's scared of heights like I'm scared of Floyd ...

Feet dragging in the grass, I approach the garage. "What if I come up?"

"To kill the bird?"

My fists tighten around the ladder. "To help you get down."

"Do I have a choice?"

I climb the ladder. As I crawl onto the roof, a robin arrows out of the maple tree right for me, veering off at the last minute with a loud screech. The baby robin has wet feathers and a stunned expression. Every now and then it flutters its wings, claws scrabbling on the shingles. No takeoff. But it's trying.

"Where's the nest?" I say.

Still crouched low, Tully nods toward a junction of three branches, where a mess of small twigs have been woven together. A head is poking over the edge, beak gaping. "The parents can't feed them while I'm on the roof," she mutters. "When I got up here, I realized I couldn't lift the bird back into the nest because I was afraid to stand up."

I slide one hand under the baby robin and lift it carefully. It blinks at me, eyes shiny. Its heartbeat thrums under my fingertips. Taking advantage of the slope of the roof, glad it's not too steep, I duck under the branches, water dripping on my shoulders, and place the bird back in the nest. Its head flops onto the twigs. Perhaps I've killed it. Tully will never forgive me.

I sidestep down the roof. "Stay on your hands and knees and crawl backward to the ladder. I'll be right behind you."

"I told you," she says, her voice shaking, "I'm afraid to move."

"I've been lifting weights—I'll catch you if you fall." I'm not nearly as confident as I sound, but she doesn't need to know that. "C'mon, you hate my guts. You don't want to have a meltdown in front of me."

With my hands—which still hurt—flat to the shingles, my feet search for the first rung of the ladder. "Okay, start backing up now."

"I can't!"

"Yes, you can." I duck as the robin does another kamikaze dive. Protecting its young. What a concept. "Tully, until you leave the roof, the robins can't feed their kids. You want two deaths on your conscience?"

The only answer is a faint moan.

"How about if I hold your ankles?" I say. "Would that help?"

Her shoulders are rigid, her nails digging into the shingles. "Can't hurt," she mumbles.

She's wearing denim cutoffs and faded pink sneakers. No socks. Her skin is cool, damp from the rain. Bones jut under my palms; blue veins wander like rivers.

With a click like a camera shutter, I fall in love with Tully Langille's ankles.

"Take it slow," I say, "little by little," and wonder who I'm talking to.

Her knee skids on the wet roof. She gives a strangled gasp. "It's okay, Tully, it's okay," I say, just like I talk to Cassie after Floyd's done his thing. "A little farther. Then I'll guide your foot to the first rung."

She's doing her best. *Respect others* ... For the first time in my life, I'm beginning to understand what that means.

She edges one knee over the gutter. I place her sneaker firmly on the rung. "Put your hands to the top of the ladder, one by one ... that's it."

Her second foot anchors itself on a lower rung. I go down a couple of rungs, then bring the first foot down one. Step-by-step we descend the ladder, until I say, "I'm on the ground now—not much longer."

As she takes the last two steps, I'm holding the sides of the ladder firm, caging her in. She's grabbing for breath, her body so close that her hair brushes my chin; it smells like Della's flowers.

I want to stand like this forever.

One pink sneaker touches the ground, tentative, then firmer. "Am I down?" Tully quavers.

I swallow and let go of the ladder. "Yep ... last foot and you're home free."

Now both her feet are on the ground. She sags against the ladder, her forehead resting on one of the rungs. "Stupid robin," she says.

I step back.

Slowly she straightens and turns around. Her eyes are a shade between green and brown, like the river when it runs under the trees in summer. Hey, who needs Wordsworth when you've got Brick MacAvoy?

She says, "I don't like you. Never have."

I take another step back. "I have to go home. Cassie needs her breakfast."

And I thought Floyd's slaps hurt.

"I haven't finished!" She jams her hands in her pockets. "Thank you for getting me down from the roof. And for putting the bird back in the nest. It was ... kind of you."

Kind. She looks at me and I look at her.

Kind Brick MacAvoy? Perfect example of an oxymoron. I go for the truth. Or at least, part of it. "I wasn't being kind."

Although was I, just maybe, giving empathy a dry run?

Nah. It was Tully's ankles.

I dig my toes into the grass, but she grips my wrist before I can run, and says, "Cassie won't starve in the next two minutes."

"I don't have to stick around and be insulted by you."

"I can't figure you out! You knocked Lorne down at school and threw rocks at Igor, but you're mostly nice to Cassie—although sometimes she goes mute when you're anywhere near. Snyder and his gang banged you up pretty bad, which means you're likely into drugs. Then today you put that little bird back in its nest like you really cared what happened to it."

I tug my arm free. "I didn't care."

Her eyes are like skewers. "You're so full of it."

In desperation, I opt for the truth. "The bird was trying so hard to fly on its own. Once I picked it up ... I guess I did care. A bit."

"*Are* you into drugs, Brick?"

Now what do I say? If I deny it, she'll start wondering if someone other than Snyder beat me up. I can't afford to have Tully Langille wondering about every bruise and scrape. There's nothing wrong with her brains—wondering could lead her straight to Floyd. I say roughly, "Just leave me alone."

"Drugs are a dead-end street! Don't you see how stupid you're being?"

"Quit preaching! And if you hate me so much, why didn't you tell your parents I'm a bully?"

Her shoulders sag. "Dad needed help with the scraping and I knew I could keep an eye on you."

"I'm not Cassie. I don't need you keeping an eye on me." Then I'm off—form lousy, breath choppy, gravel the only thing that's flying.

8.4 [*Hope is the thing with feathers—that perches in the soul* ... Emily Dickinson. American poet, 1830-86. I'm showing off.]

I MAKE Cassie a late breakfast. I'm not hungry. Do the weights, increasing the reps. Practice stances, blocks, punches, and kicks. Focus. Focus. Focus. Stare at the five principles until I can say them backward and upside down. Shower. Clean the bathroom. Take Cassie to town.

We buy a box of Smarties at Sobeys. At the bakery, we're in luck because they just took a tray of chocolate chip cookies out of the oven. I ask the lady behind the counter if I can buy a dozen and explain what we want to do. Once she's spread the cookies on wax paper for us, I tip out the Smarties and let Cassie choose the colors she wants. Then we press three Smarties into each of the soft, warm cookies. I use red, yellow, and green on mine, traffic-light colors, just like I used to with Kendra. Cassie goes for purple, blue, and orange. After we go outside, we each eat one, the chocolate melting in our mouths.

While Cassie's leafing through picture books at the library, I find a book about the treasures of Afghanistan from the time of the Silk Road, which is a road that stretched all the way from China to Babylon 2000 years ago. Think about it. No ATVs.

Near the front of the book, there's a photo of a statue of the Buddha, the clay a warm, soft brown, his robe in long curves. He has this half-smile, like he knows something I don't.

There's also a photo of a thin gold chain that went around a princess's ankle.

Not much point in falling in love with Tully Langille's ankles, knees, or elbows.

FLOYD BRINGS Opal flowers that night, a big bunch of red roses wrapped in cellophane. She sniffs them and kisses him, rubbing up against him. Then she puts the roses in a crystal vase on the coffee table in the living room and they go upstairs.

Is Opal in love with Floyd? Worse—is Floyd in love with Opal? If that's love, it's all yours.

BY NOW, Cassie's used to me running in the mornings after Floyd leaves for work, so she doesn't fuss. I haven't told Docker I run every day except Sunday—my secret. The way it makes me feel—like there's hope, like there's something I can do right—is my secret too.

When I poke the backs of my calves, they're tight. Muscles. I have muscles.

It's raining today, real rain, but I don't care. I kind of like it, the drops cool on my face, my T-shirt wet on my skin. I take Swamp Road again, going farther until I reach a clear-cut. A few spindly birch and maples, tufts of leaves at the top, dead spruce boughs strewn everywhere. No place left for a robin to build a nest.

Just before I woke up I was dreaming about Tully. She was stirring yellow paint over the fire pit in her backyard, her hair as bright as the flames. Then she smiled at me the way she smiles at Cassie, nothing held back. The dream moved to her ankles. Censor the rest.

Three and a half months ago. Recess on a damp day in April. Five girls are circling Tully in the schoolyard.

"Rolf Langille's not your real father."

"Who's your real father, Tully?"

"Why didn't he marry your mother?"

"Didn't want to, did he? Because then he'd have you for a kid."

"Like, who'd want you?"

"When are going to quit riding that stupid bike and behave like a girl?"

Tully's face is red. "Rolf Langille is my real father."

"Bastard on a bicycle, that's you." They giggle.

Tully says, loud enough that everyone in the schoolyard can hear, "Rolf adopted me in December, Langille is my last name, and if behaving like a girl means being like you, I'd rather drive my bike off the wharf."

One of the girls sticks her face into Tully's. "Bitch," she says.

The chorus starts up again. "Have you looked in a mirror lately?"

"I wouldn't put that T-shirt on my worst enemy."

"No wonder the boys don't want anything to do with you."

Tully spits the f-word at them and marches away. She always looks taller than she is because she holds herself so straight.

When it comes to spite, girls win hands down.

I DON'T know who her biological father is, or why she didn't keep his name. I should have asked her while I had her trapped on the roof. Even then, I'm almost sure she wouldn't have told me.

I turn around. The clear-cut's starting to get to me.

I walk the hill on #539 past MacTaggart's, then slow-jog to our road. Glenn's just leaving his place wearing a rain jacket, Igor on the leash. The dog looks mournful. I bet half an hour with Caramel would cheer him up.

Glenn hears me coming. Warily he looks back at the house, where the VW is parked askew in the driveway.

I stop, panting. He braces himself. Igor skulks in the ditch. "Glenn," I say, between breaths, "I won't be bullying you again. You or Igor."

Sure, I'm high on endorphins, which is why I use the real word, *bullying*. But it's not just hormones speaking. It's the truth pushing its way out: *I will not bully Glenn Semple anymore.* By telling him, I make it truer.

No such word. True is true.

The wary look comes my way. "Why?"

Because his father offered me a freebie? Because I looked deep into Igor's eyes and all I saw was sadness? Or is it because those pennies and nickels clinking in the dust made me feel lower than bilge?

"Doesn't matter why."

He flicks a quick punch to my chest. Instantly I drop into front stance, fingers and thumb folded into a fist that's headed straight for him.

No contact! screams through my brain. The fist stops in midair.

I drop my arm. He can't stop his second punch, which jars my ribs. This time I stand still, breathing hard, nails digging into my palms.

"Guess what, Igor?" he says. "Brick's reformed. Can we believe him?"

"It's true!" First time I've admitted to being a bully and he's giving me a hard time?

"Hang out the balloons. Bring on the brass band. But let's wait six months, just to be sure."

I'm itching to slap him up the side of the head, and maybe it shows. He takes a step back, bouncing on the gravel like he's a boxer, his fists jabbing the air.

While Horton was hatching the egg, he had this annoying habit of insisting he would never, ever, break his word. If Horton can stay the course, so can I. I swipe rain and sweat from my forehead, turn my back on Glenn and Igor, and start jogging down the road.

Tully is pedaling her bike toward us, top speed. I'm not in the mood for Tully Langille. Eyes front, mentally blocking my ears, I run faster.

She flashes past me.

A couple of minutes later, I look back. Tully and Glenn are facing each other, and even through the raindrops I can see they're arguing. I run faster, reach our driveway, and race past the tattered spruce trees and the chunks of granite.

When I lie, people believe me; when I tell the truth, they don't.

9.1 [white knight III]

CASSIE AND I spend the afternoon in town at the library and the mall. Back at the house, she wants chicken fingers for supper, so that's what I cook, along with egg noodles, frozen corn, and raw carrots—is this health food or what? Dirty dishes are piled in the sink, because Floyd and Opal ate home for once. Floyd's in the living room working on a jigsaw; Opal had an appointment in Collings Head, so she's gone.

After I daub the batter with sweet-and-sour sauce and squirt ketchup all over, Cassie decides she wants to eat in her room.

"Wait a second," I say, "and I'll carry your plate upstairs."

I turn away to take my own chicken fingers off the cookie sheet. I'm a barbecue sauce guy myself.

An almighty crash in the living room. I whip around. Cassie's not in the kitchen.

Wood scrapes on wood, followed by a crack like a BB gun. Cassie screeches.

Like a sprinter from the starting gun, I'm into the living room. Broken plate on the floor, sweet-and-sour sauce and ketchup slithering down the leg of the card table, jigsaw pieces scattered all over. Cassie is crouched against the coffee table. On her cheek, red, the imprint of Floyd's hand.

Floyd hit her. He hit Cassie.

He picks her up by the elbows, holding her chest-high, and shakes her as though she's a rag doll.

I take two steps forward. Everything in slow motion. Like I weigh 500 pounds.

The roses are still on the coffee table. I wrap both hands around them, toss them to one side, watch them land in the ketchup. I pick up the crystal vase. Can't throw it in case I hit Cassie.

Water slops over my hand. I swing the vase in an arc. The rest of the water slaps Floyd in the face and drips from Cassie's curls. He drops her like she's a piece of garbage.

She bangs into the corner of the coffee table. Her knees hit the floor.

Another two steps. I'm gripping the vase by the throat. I'm gonna bash his brains in.

My sneaker skids off the broken plate, which is slippery with sauce. I glance down. Fatal.

His fist misses my gut, ploughs into my ribcage. Off balance, I flail at him with the vase. It hits him on the arm. *Thunk.*

Somehow I keep hold of it. Raise it to crack his head open.

I don't even see his fist. It slams into my shoulder, knocks me backward. The vase goes flying, hits the couch, and bounces to the floor. He lunges at me, twists my shirt, jerks me upright, and slaps me. Once, twice.

My eyes are watering. Frantically I try to anchor my feet, to focus.

Two more vicious slaps. Through a blur of pain and, yep, tears, I see Cassie scramble to her feet and head for Floyd, her nails like claws, her teeth bared.

Then he sees her. His face, like hers, is a mask of fury. I shove him in the chest, jolt him sideways with my hip, and surge toward her. "No, Cassie, no!"

When I pick her up, she struggles, kicking out at me. A sneaker nails me in the belly. "Stop it!"

I hold her at arms' length. Across the corner of the coffee table my eyes meet Floyd's. His chest's heaving like he just ran the length of the road. He says, "You tell her she should never— ever—turn on me again. Is that clear?"

"You hit her! She's four years old."

"Did you hear me?"

Cassie has stopped struggling. I hug her close to my chest. "Have you hit her before?"

"And tell her to stay out of my way."

I feel like I just swallowed a whole shitload of frozen corn. This isn't the first time he's hit Cassie. Where the hell have I been?

Her crooning to herself in the backyard about messes and Bang-ups ...

"You *have* hit her before," I say in a dead voice. "Why would you do that? She doesn't remind you of Thaddeus. Not like me."

"Get her out of my sight! Then clean up this mess."

We both need to be out of his sight. I carry Cassie upstairs, feeling his gaze drill into my back. In her room, I sit down on the bed and swipe my wet cheeks with the back of one hand.

Horrified, I realize she's crying, tears brimming on her lashes, spilling down her face, splashing onto my bare arm. I put both arms around her and draw her close. She huddles into my chest. By now she's sobbing, this little kid who hardly ever cries.

I remember the morning she spilled the milk, how she cowered into her seat. I remember the day I was going to leave her home with Floyd, her face dead-white. I also remember how she's reverted to sucking her thumb. All those clues, and I ignored every one of them. How could I have been so stupid?

I can't leave her alone with him ever again. Not for an hour. Not even for five minutes.

But that's not all. Like a sledgehammer to the chest, I realize something else. I can't leave here the day I turn sixteen. Leave her with Floyd? With me gone, she'd be the only one left for him to knock around. She'd be his pressure valve. His punching bag.

I'm tied to her. We're in this together and no way out.

My little sister. Who came to my rescue.

I rub my cheek on her hair. I love Cassie.

Well yeah, of course I do. I just never put it into words before.

The walls crowd closer. Rain patters on the roof like little feet. I shut my eyes, rocking her back and forth.

9.2 ["Dead Man Walking"]

EVENTUALLY CASSIE stops crying; I pass her a Kleenex and she blows her nose. "How many times has Floyd hit you, Cassie?"

She unfolds four fingers on her right hand and holds them up.

"Why didn't you tell me?"

"You said not to."

"I didn't mean—I just didn't want you telling anyone else about Floyd. But you could have told me."

"You said not to tell," she repeats stubbornly.

"Oh, God, Cassie, I'm sorry—I've screwed up big time. I should've realized what was happening, but I didn't think he'd ever hit you ... how dumb is that? I'm *sorry*."

"Make me Cream of Wheat?" she says.

Comfort food. I go downstairs, walking around cold chicken fingers and wilted roses on my way to the kitchen, and make her a big bowl of Cream of Wheat with maple syrup. She eats some of it, then falls asleep, clutching Rover.

I slap peanut butter on bread and eat it standing by the sink.

Roses and food go in the compost bucket, plate shards into the garbage. Jigsaw pieces—turquoise pond daubed with ketchup—back on the card table. A bucket of soapy water takes care of the rest of the ketchup and the sweet-and-sour sauce. I don't care if I ever see a chicken finger again.

After dumping the water down the sink and rinsing out the bucket, I go back upstairs. Behind Floyd's bedroom door, I can hear canned laughter from the small TV they keep on their bureau. I'd bet the stash he won't tell Opal what happened tonight.

I fall down on my bed, intending to read, and wake up at three with the light still on. Across the hall, Cassie's crying again.

I stumble into her room and hold her while she tells me about the monster who was chasing her, his axe dripping rose petals that turned into blood. After I cuddle her for a while, she goes back to sleep. But now I'm wide-awake.

Back in my room, I take out a piece of paper and a pen, and stare at the paper for a long time. Stray thoughts meander through my brain. Like, I didn't use karate against Floyd last night. Like, am I nuts to prefer punches to slaps, slaps that make me feel as if I'm Cassie's age again? Like, how can he hit his four-year-old daughter?

No answer to that one. So I switch gears to the question I've been avoiding ever since I realized that I can't leave home when

I'm sixteen because I've been landed with a new job twenty-four seven, no pay—to keep Cassie safe, to protect her the best I can. The question being, do I have any other options?

Leave anyway and take her with you.

And support both of us on my savings, which at the moment, counting future lawn mowing, amount to just over $800? Daycare alone would eat that up in no time. Add grub and a roof over our heads? Can't be done.

Rat on Floyd. Tell the cops. Or the social worker who has an office upstairs in the mall.

Yeah, and then what would happen? Assuming they believed me—big assumption—we'd be caught up in the system. They'd take Cassie away, put her in a foster home. I'd go somewhere else, because who'd want a teenager with a rep as a bully?

Cassie, living with strangers? She might hate it and I wouldn't be there to run interference. I've

heard horror stories
about foster homes. Maybe
I wouldn't even be allowed
to visit her.

If they didn't believe
us—if they believed the
Salesman-of-the-Year's
version—there's risk and
then there's pounding nails
in your own coffin.

Tell Marigold and Rolf. They'd head for the
authorities, I know they
would.

Stay, keep it a secret, Cassie turned four in June.
and make sure Floyd She can leave home when
never gets the chance she's sixteen. Sixteen
to hit her again. years minus four years
equals twelve years equals
infinity.

Infinity. Heavier than Everest. Dryer than the Gobi.

I DON'T go for my morning run.

Cassie has bruises on her knees and another one on her back. I won't take her to Marigold's. I don't want to go near the dojo. And what's the point of mowing Della's lawn? The savings account isn't worth the paper it's written on.

I won't even be able to get a proper job when I turn sixteen. Tim Hortons won't let me keep Cassie behind the counter while I work my shift, and I can't dump her at one of the tables for eight hours. Cassie behind the cash register at Sobeys or Shoppers? I don't think so.

I'm stuck. No way out.

We watch TV all morning. Floyd threw out the puzzle; the card table is folded against the wall.

I was planning on asking Docker for bigger weights today. I'd better leave a message on his machine. Tell him I'm quitting. Let's face it, I'll never dare use karate against Floyd. He'd grind me into hamburger, and then where would Cassie be?

Three times I pick up the phone.

Three times I put it down again.

Docker Lonergan's been decent to me. I'm not sure why, but that's not the point. Am I going to do my coward-gig and leave a message on an answering machine that I'm quitting? Or will I— *respecting others*—tell him face-to-face?

I'd rather stack ten woodpiles.

Either way, he'll be royally pissed. Quickly I look up his home number and punch the digits. One ring, two—me in a funk in case he answers. Finally the message clicks on, then the beep.

"Docker," I say, "I'm not coming to the dojo anymore. Sorry. Thanks. Oh. It's Brick." Then I push End, my heart banging away as if I just ran uphill full speed.

At twelve thirty, the phone rings. One of Floyd's rules is that you always answer the telephone. I pick it up like it's a rabid ferret.

Marigold says, "Do you both like corn on the cob? We thought we'd do a corn boil this evening. Barbecue some hot dogs. It's too hot to cook indoors."

"We can't come today."

There's a pause. "Are you all right?"

I make an effort to talk normal. "I'm fine. But we can't come."

Cassie gloms herself to my leg. "Today's the day we go see Caramel."

How does she know it's Thursday? "We can't, Cassie ... sorry, Marigold, but not today."

"I want to see Caramel!" Cassie grabs for the phone.

"We're not going!"

She starts wailing. "Bye, Marigold," I say, and slam the phone into its cradle. "I'm not going to Docker's dojo anymore, Cassie. So we're staying home."

"No more play-store?" She wails louder, stomping her feet and slapping at my thigh.

Her slaps hurt. Why wouldn't they? She's seen me slapped and she's been slapped. Over the racket, I say, "We'll go to Mac-Taggart's and you can buy some candy, okay?"

"Caramel's not allowed in MacTaggart's."

"Gummi bears."

The wail subsides to a snuffle. "I love Caramel," she says.

"I know you do. You'll see him another day."

I dress her in long pants and a long-sleeved shirt so no one at the store will see the bruises. After I take some money from the jar in the pantry, we're out the door. At the end of our drive-way, I stop the ATV to check for trucks.

Cassie screams, "Caramel!"

Tully and Caramel are walking toward us, Caramel on a red leash. I switch to the foot brake and wrap one arm around Cassie as she squirms on the seat.

"Down, Brick—I want *down!*"

Caramel yaps, wagging his tail. Tully's staring at me, her mouth set, her eyes as green and hard as sea-glass. I tighten my grip on Cassie. "Quit wriggling."

"No harm in her patting Caramel," Tully says. "Don't you let her do anything that's any fun?"

I let go. Cassie slides down onto the side of the road, then embraces Caramel. If she had a tail, it'd be wagging. I say, "We can't stop long."

"I'm gonna stay with Caramel," Cassie says.

"No, you're not!"

"I thought you were leaving her with us today," Tully says.

"No."

Cassie screeches, "I am *so* staying with Caramel!"

"She can stay the rest of the day," Tully says. "Mom likes having her, and Cassie likes being at our place. It gives her a break."

From me. *Thanks, Tully. Thanks loads.* I know my limits, though; I can't cope with the ATV, the river trail, and Cassie in major-tantrum mode. "Okay," I say grudgingly. "I'll pick her up before supper. Be a good girl, Cassie."

She gives me her most angelic smile. "Yep," she says.

Twelve more years? I'll be in the loony bin.

I watch while the three of them cross the road and head down the slope to the river.

Now what?

Can't stay here.

Can't go home. Opal said she'd be back before lunch. She might notice Cassie's missing. Although, what are the odds?

Can't go to the dojo. I've quit.

Can't bully Glenn Semple. What kind of an idiot was I telling him he was off my list?

Can't go into town. Just my luck to meet up with Docker and/or Snyder and/or his gang.

In desperation, I decide to go to MacTaggart's anyway and pick up the latest ATV magazine. That's when I realize Della is standing at the end of her driveway, beckoning to me with her clippers.

If I was in love with all of Tully, not just her ankles, I'd let her mow Della's grass. And why not? I don't need the money now. I'm stuck here until infinity runs out.

A totally useless fact: in four billion years, the sun will become a red giant and we'll all fry. I roar down Della's driveway, pull up behind the shed, and turn off the ATV.

She's followed me down the driveway. As if our last conversation was three minutes ago, not three days, she says, "Come and take a look at the stone wall. It needs rebuilding."

We walk down the slope and contemplate the wall that edges the woods. It's a jumble of rocks more than a wall. "First step is to pull it down," Della says. She looks at me doubtfully. "Even if you're interested, I'm not sure you can handle it—possibly it's a man's job."

"I've been lifting weights."

"Let's give it a try. Can I trust you to stop if it's too much?" I nod again. "All right, I'll find you some gloves."

When she comes back, she's also carrying a pair of old steel-toed boots. She holds them out. "Try these on. It looks as though they'll fit you."

Men's boots.

I take them from her. She hitches her bundle of hair, her gaze far away. "They belonged to my brother, Wendell—he was your typical reckless adolescent who thought he was immortal. After eating some hallucinogenic mushrooms, he decided to race his motorbike on the highway. He drove off the bridge at Collings Harbor and drowned."

"I'm sorry," I say.

"It broke Agnes's heart."

More than Agnes's, by the look of it. I take off my sneakers and lace the boots. A bit loose, but they'll protect my feet if I drop a rock. Wearing a dead guy's boots ... never done that before.

In her normal, no-nonsense voice, Della tells me where she wants the rocks piled, and I go to it. I soon get into a rhythm, my muscles gradually warming up, sort of like running. Doubt if I could have done this two weeks ago. The rocks are heavy, but I'm moving them, sorting and piling them according to size and shape.

Best I've felt the last twenty-four hours.

Mid-afternoon, Della brings me a glass of water, checks what I've done, then gazes at me thoughtfully. "You're stronger than you look," she says. "I have a pamphlet on building a stone wall that I printed off the Internet. Would you read it before you start rebuilding? If you do the grass tomorrow, you could work on the wall over the weekend."

"Providing Cassie can stay at Marigold's."

"Let me know."

If I still needed the money, I'd be one happy dude. I drain the water glass, pass it back, and heave more rocks off the wall, big ones I wasn't sure I could manage. Then I up-end the ones on the bottom row. By now, it looks like a minor earthquake hit the backyard. But Della's happy. "I'll warn Agnes not to walk out here," she says briskly. "Shall I pay you when you're finished, so we can total the hours?"

A nice guy, a decent guy, would ask her right now if Tully could mow the lawn. But if I save more money, don't I have more options? I could quit school the December I turn sixteen and get a job in Halifax. Put Cassie in daycare. Or catch the train to Toronto and ask Kendra to keep us until I find a job there.

Sure. And deal with kidnapping charges in my spare time. If I took Cassie to Halifax—or Toronto—even Opal would eventually realize we were gone. Floyd sure would. No punching bags.

Just the same, I'm going to bank every cent I can get my hands on.

Della says patiently, "Is that all right, Brick?"

"Oh. Yeah."

"I'll see you tomorrow."

She walks away, ramrod-straight in her baggy trousers. I leave the boots in the shed, drive across the road again, and tuck the ATV into the trees by Rolf's garage. I should repaint it in a camouflage pattern.

9.3 [tattletale]

THE LID of the barbecue is closed, a pot is steaming over the coals in the brick fire pit, reminding me of my dream. When I walk into the kitchen, Caramel runs at me, wiggles his butt, and licks my hand. The ceiling fan is whirring. Marigold's leaning against the counter while Rolf is stationed by the sink like a soldier on duty. Tully's sitting at the table. They all stare at me. No one says hello.

"What's up?" I say. "Where's Cassie?"

Marigold says, "She fell asleep in front of the TV. She seemed tired today."

She's entitled. Seeing as how Floyd did a number on her yesterday. If I said that, what would happen? Nerves are crawling under my skin.

Rolf says, spacing his words, "Are you a bully, Brick? Or am I out to lunch?"

My turn to stare. At him, then at Tully. She raises her chin, her cheeks flushed. She must have weaseled the truth out of Glenn yesterday.

I just about spit the words at her. "You saw me with Glenn yesterday morning. Why'd you wait this long to tell your dad?"

"I told him right after Glenn told me. But then Dad got called to a power outage in Collings Head after a truck hit a light pole, and he was out until late." She stands up, her cheeks a deeper shade of red. "What does the timing matter? You've been bullying Glenn for months. Right here on the road. He's my *friend*. Not that *you'd* understand that word."

I wonder if he told her how I made him cry.

She says flatly, "I should have twigged to you that day by the ladder."

Rolf tugs his ear. "I'd trust Tully's word on anything—but I sure didn't want to believe her yesterday. I was on the early shift today, so I didn't have the chance to tell Marigold until an hour ago ... I don't do anything without talking to Marigold."

I wish he'd hurry up.

"You haven't answered the question," he says.

The question. Oh yeah. Am I a bully.

I go for the truth. Well, I hope it's the truth. "I quit."

"You've bullied Glenn and the Meisner kid and the Donovans."

"Yes. But—"

"So you're a bully at school, at the store, and right here on the road. Other places too, likely. I told you I can't abide strong-arm stuff. Guess you didn't hear me."

"I did. I heard you. Like I said, I'm trying to quit."

"Quit? Punching a kid out isn't the same as dragging on a cig-arette," he says. "Do you bully your sister?"

"No!"

"Bullies pick on kids who are smaller than them. Weaker. More vulnerable."

"I've never touched Cassie."

Because of where I'm standing, I can see that Cassie's woken up; she's sitting on the couch, rubbing her eyes.

Marigold says, "Brick, I hate this ... I feel as though we're put-ting you on trial. But there's something I have to ask—did you throw rocks at Igor?"

"I told Glenn I'd never do it again."

She bites her lip. She's disappointed in me. Makes me feel like I've swallowed broken glass.

"By God, boy," Rolf says softly, "if I ever see you picking on anyone, kid or dog, I'll have the cops onto you so fast you won't see them coming."

"I keep telling you, I'm not doing it anymore."

But he's not finished. "I asked you once if you do drugs. Sny-der and his gang make a habit of beating up kids who double-cross them on deals. When you told us you fell off your ATV and banged up your face—you were lying, weren't you?"

Panic streaks up and down my spine. Brain in overdrive and no solution in sight. Any thoughts of telling Rolf and Marigold about Floyd are dead in the water. They wouldn't believe me; they'd think I was trying to pass the buck.

. I shoot a look at Cassie. She's standing beside the couch now, her thumb in her mouth. *Keep it there, kid.*

"Okay," I say, "so it was Snyder. But—"

"That does it," Rolf says heavily, pushing away from the counter and looking over at Marigold. Her face is pale.

"We still want Cassie to come here," she says. "As often as she likes."

"But you're not welcome," Rolf says.

No time to block that one. It rocks me clear to my toes.

Caramel has fallen asleep draped over Rolf's socked feet. The ceiling fan is still whirring. "Fine," I say. "I'll take Cassie home right now."

"We'd like her to stay for supper," Marigold says.

"Then I'll pick her up at seven thirty. If you can handle me driving into your yard."

"One of us will walk her home," Marigold says.

"No!"

"Why not?" Rolf demands.

"Opal doesn't like visitors." I gotta get out of here. "Seven thirty," I say and I'm out the door and running for the ATV.

If the hot dogs were already on the barbecue, they'll be charcoal dogs.

I can't blame anyone but me for what just happened.

9.4 [scat]

THE RIVER trail is shaded and cool. Ferns slap the wheels of the ATV. When I turn off the ignition, their bruised scent clogs the air. For a long while I stare at the dark brown water, at the way it sweeps toward the rocks, breaks up into foam, rejoins the current. Always moving, always going somewhere. Doesn't it know it'll get swallowed by the sea?

In the sixteenth century they used to pile rocks on criminals, one by one, more and more of them until the guy's ribs caved in and all his bones broke and eventually he died. *Peine forte et dure* they called it.

After a while, I drive farther downriver and park off-trail. Ducking dead spruce boughs sharp-pointed as knives, stumbling over rocks, slipping on the moss, I shove my way through the woods until I see the roof of the old hunting shack. It's covered with moss too. No glass in the windows. Hinges loose on the door, which groans as I push it open.

So many trees surround it that the light inside is almost green. It smells musty, as though long ago something crawled under the floorboards to die.

I sit down on one of the two wooden chairs and rest my fore-head on my hands. I can still hear the river. Under that sound—which never stops—there's only silence.

I don't know how long I sit there. Until I can't stand my own thoughts any longer, I guess. I run my fingers over the stubble on my head and look around.

A wooden table, two chairs, two bunks, no mattresses, an oil drum with a rusty black chimney. Cobwebs furring the corners. Little piles of raccoon shit everywhere.

Deep inside, something stirs to life. Slats on the windows would keep the animals out. The door hinges could be tightened. A broom would do wonders for the floor.

I wonder if the roof leaks.

I'll need a place to go if Cassie's going to spend any amount of time at Rolf's. And this could be my place. Nothing to do with Floyd. Nothing to do with anyone but me. Me and Cassie.

AT SEVEN thirty, Marigold is waiting outside on the step with Cassie. As I turn off the ignition, she says, "I'm sorry it's worked out this way, Brick."

She does look sorry. She doesn't look as though she's about to change her mind, though. "Me too," I say.

"Bring her over anytime ... but please call first."

If I'm going to work on Della's wall, I'll need a place for Cassie on the weekend. I swallow my pride. "Could I leave her with you on Saturday?"

She nods. "Rolf's on day shift then, so I'll be around."

I thank her, then Cassie and I drive back to the house. We've got the place to ourselves. As soon as we go inside, she says, "Did you throw rocks at Igor?"

Oh man. "Once or twice. I'll never do it again."

"You gonna throw rocks at Caramel?"

"No. I'm hungry ... go watch TV for a while."

Twin blue lasers point straight at me. "You better not throw rocks at Caramel," she says, "or I'll beat you up."

Supper tastes like raccoon shit. No message on the machine from Docker.

Dodging around the kitchen table and chairs, I flick out punches, ward them off, knees bent, my socked feet skidding on the pine boards. Then I lose my balance on the side kick, knock over a chair, and nearly follow it to the floor.

I can't do anything right.

9.5 [painstaking]

ONCE FLOYD'S left for work on Friday, I hurry downstairs. Opal's at the kitchen table with her coffee and the morning paper. I say, "I'm out for the day—I'll be back at five. I'm leaving Cassie home."

"I have an appointment this afternoon."

"Cancel it."

"I don't know what's gotten into you lately, Brick, but I don't care for it."

"Do you want to know what Floyd did two days ago? He hit Cassie. It's not the first time, either."

"He wouldn't do that." But she looks uneasy.

"I saw him!"

Her mouth tightens. "Pete's giving him a hard time at work."

"And that's supposed to make it okay? Opal, I'm never leaving her alone with him again. If I see him make one move toward her, I'll call the cops."

I say this with such conviction that *I'm* almost convinced. Opal shifts in her chair. "You mustn't do that. I'll watch over her today."

Well, that was easy. "I took some new DVDs out of the library for Cassie. They're on the coffee table." Then I shove two pieces of bread in the toaster and throw together a sandwich for lunch.

At Della's, I park the ATV behind the shed; I brought it so Opal would think I've gone to town. As Della steps down from the deck, she gives it a pointed look. "Walking is becoming obsolete," she says. "Did the pamphlet make sense?"

I studied it while I was eating the toast. "I think so."

"The gloves and boots are in the shed. A shovel and a crowbar are in there as well. The bathroom's to the left of the kitchen, and there's water in the refrigerator."

I cut the grass first, to get that out of the way. Then I take the tools out of the shed, lay them on the grass, and stare at the tumble of rocks. All different shapes and sizes of rocks. Can I do this?

Panic is not an option.

I flip through the pamphlet again.

Half an hour later, four stakes mark the corners of the wall-to-be, cord pulled tight from stake to stake so the wall will be straight. Some of the footing has heaved, so I work on making it level, using the bumpiest stones. You bury the bumps, keeping the flat side up.

The footing is two feet wide and two stones wide. The wall has to be the same width with a slight dip to the center. Like the Shaker round. And I thought *that* was a challenge.

Each layer of the wall is called a *course*. Yep, building a stone wall has a language all its own.

You use the heaviest rocks for the first course, because then you don't have to lift them very high. When you lay stone on stone, no wobble is permitted. Shimming, however, is permitted.

Hard to avoid wobble. Harder still to make the first layer level. But every time *you're so dumb, kiddo*, starts to play, I blank it out.

When Della comes out to inspect, the first course is finished and I've just started sorting rocks for the second. The wall is less than six inches high. I say with a touch of desperation, "Rebuilding a wall is way slower than tearing it down."

She smiles her non-post-office smile. "You've discovered a profound truth—a pity the world's dictators won't pay any attention. It looks fine, Brick. I'd rather have a good job than a rushed job."

She makes me feel okay, the same way Rolf did when I was scraping and painting.

I don't want to think about Rolf.

SATURDAY, OPAL and Floyd sleep in. I leave Opal a note saying we've gone to the playground for the day, and drive to Marigold's to drop off Cassie. It's cool, so Cassie's wearing her long pants again.

Smiling at Cassie, Marigold says, "I need you to entertain Caramel, because Tully's spending the day with Glenn and his parents in Halifax."

Envy that Tully's in Halifax, relief that she's out of my hair for today, jealousy that she's with Glenn ... *jealousy?*

"I'm working on Della's wall," I say clumsily, "and it's supposed to rain on Monday. Can I leave her until after supper today? And tomorrow morning until I finish up? Della doesn't like kids."

"If we need to go to Sobeys after Rolf's shift today, we'll take her with us. Tomorrow morning's fine."

I feel like a worm. "Thank you," I say, wishing she'd smile at me.

Then I drive the ATV to Della's, parking it behind the shed again. The grass is trim and tidy, and the first course looks as if it'll still be in place in 2050. I settle down to work.

When I woke up this morning, I wanted to go for a run. Decided to save my energy. But I take a couple of breaks during the day, doing karate moves to loosen up. My balance is improving. It really is.

No word from Docker. Doesn't he care I've quit?

By dusk I finish the fifth course, carefully placing tie stones that reach from front to back and help anchor the wall.

I feel like I just ran five marathons. But the wall actually looks like a wall.

10.1 [buzzed]

SUNDAY, WHEN I deliver Cassie to Marigold's, Tully is outside with Caramel. I wonder if she had a good time in Halifax with Glenn and why I give a rat's ass. Hard to believe I ever had my hands wrapped around her ankles.

"I'm working on Della's stone wall," I say.

"I saw you mowing her grass the other day," she says, her voice zero on the friendly scale.

So that's the end of that conversation.

Because I'm sore all over, it takes a while to get moving at Della's. But then I find the right rhythm; just after midday, I lay the last stone on the top course of the wall. Carefully I replace Wendell's boots on the shelf in the shed. What a major waste, to die in a stupid accident when you're buzzed.

Neatly I tuck the laces inside the boots and leave them on

the shelf. Outside, the garden is a riot of scent and color—blue, pink, orange, and yellow.

As I walk back down the slope, a hummingbird zips toward a shaggy red flower. I stand and inspect the wall. Rocks overlapping nicely, no vertical fissures to weaken it, corners as square as I could make them, and flat stones lined up along the top.

Della is pleased, and says so. In the envelope she passes me are six red bills, fifty-dollar bills, plus thirty dollars for the lawn.

"That's too much," I say. "I was learning on the job."

"If I thought it was too much, I wouldn't have given it to you."

"Oh." Which is my fallback word whenever I don't know what else to say.

We part the best of friends.

Best implies comparison, which implies more than one.

TULLY'S IN the yard again when I arrive to pick up Cassie. I wish she'd get lost.

She walks up to me, her face sober. "I need to talk to you for a minute."

"I'm in a hurry."

"Cassie has bruises on her knees. I saw them when she was in the bathroom. I asked her how she got them, but she wouldn't answer ... clammed up the way she does when you're around. Did you have anything to do with it? Because if you did, I have to tell Dad."

A huge tiredness settles on me, as though someone's piling rocks on my shoulders and doesn't know when to stop. Year after year of living a lie, of living in terror of the man who's my father ... and now Tully thinks I'm responsible for the bruises on my sister.

Moving like a machine, I walk around Tully, pick Cassie up, put her on the seat, climb on the ATV myself, and we drive home.

I SPEND the rest of Sunday making sure Cassie and Floyd don't end up in the same room. In her bedroom, we build a tent out of blankets; after I cook supper for the two of us, we have a picnic under the tent. Then I flake out on her bed while she plays with her plastic farm animals. Right now, if someone asked me to jog across the hall, I don't think I could.

Rolf doesn't come pounding on our door.

MONDAY MORNING, once Floyd's out of the way, I go for a run in the rain. A gap of four days and already I've lost speed and wind. Although it's tempting to use some of Della's money for a pair of expensive running shoes, I can get by with the ones I'm wearing. When I bank my pay, I'll be in the four-figure range.

Not that it'll matter how much money I have, if Tully has told Rolf about the bruises. They'll take Cassie away, and who cares what happens after that?

No sign of Rolf all day. No social workers. No cop car in the driveway, red and blue lights flashing. I start to hope that maybe, just maybe, Tully kept her lips clamped.

Early Tuesday I run again, my sneakers still damp from yesterday. Near the bridge I pass Glenn and Igor. I wave at Glenn, to let him know there are no hard feelings because he told Tully I bullied him. Also, that I'm not going to break my word about leaving him alone. He doesn't wave back.

Igor cocks his head. I swear he'd like to be running with me. Now there's a thought. Bet I could learn a thing or two about running from Igor.

As if I'm an addict who can't help himself, I practice blocks, kicks, and elbow-strikes behind the garage after my run. Speed, ferocity, and power—I like those words.

Opal isn't feeling good, so she sends me to town to pick up a prescription at the drugstore and to deliver some mail to Floyd. Cassie stays home. I put the garbage out before I leave. Docker's dropped me like I don't exist.

No, Brick. You're the one who dropped Docker. Remember?

Why do I keep practicing? So I won't miss him? Him and the dojo? Or because I'm pissed off at him because he hasn't bothered to ask why I quit?

Now that the wall's finished, I'll have more time to read; I could go to The Laughing Loon for my free book while I'm in town.

I could. I doubt I will.

At the bank I deposit the cash Della gave me, then pick up the prescription at the drugstore. I'll drive to the dealership; that way I can make a quick escape. The ATV is parked behind Shoppers.

Snyder McIsaac is poking around in the carry-bag. "Hey!" I shout.

Taking his time, he turns around, tucking his thumbs in his belt. His waist is as puffy as the bread dough at the bakery. "Lookit who's here."

He's not quite as tall as me but he packs way more weight. On skates, he's a slugger, known to fight dirty. I stick the prescription in my pocket, pulses drumming. He's alone.

"Neat buzz cut, dude," he says, and walks closer, flat-footed as a black duck.

My feet anchor themselves. I skip the bow. He jabs his fist at my face. My left forearm manages to deflect it, rising block, strictly amateur. My right elbow ploughs his ribs. My knee rams his thigh.

Hands in front of my face and shoulders hunched, I say, superpolite, "I'm glad you like it."

Snyder lacks a sense of humor. He charges, both fists flying. I block one, miss the next—*whump* in the gut and I'm floundering. For a couple of seconds, I panic. He'll crucify me.

Like the boxers Floyd watches on TV, I dance backward, to the left, to the right. He lumbers after me. Mouth a thin line, he aims for my belly, aims hard.

Downward block, *gedan barai*, then a reverse punch that— miracles of miracles—hits the target. He grunts in surprise and— I hope—pain.

I'm laughing inside and likely it shows. He surges forward, bashing at me, face, belly, wherever he thinks he can land one. I block half of them, dodge most of the rest, slam him with elbows and knees wherever there's an opening. And once, just once, I land a punch that has power behind it, power from four days of building a rock wall and the prospect of twelve years stuck in Hilchey Bay with the likes of Snyder McIsaac.

Oh yeah, it's pain this time.

My brain's working top speed. He's heavier than me, and his goons could show up anytime. He's also off-balance. I plant my weight on one foot, lift the other knee, and kick to the side with vicious force. My heel thwacks his knee. Rotten form—good thing Docker isn't here—but Snyder staggers, scrabbling at the air, then thuds to the pavement. That's when I jump on the ATV. Key in the ignition and I roar out of there.

I'm still laughing inside, laughing like a mad fool.

I did it. I got the better of him. Was it respectful to kick him harder than was necessary? To inflict, let's be honest, maximum pain? Probably not. Do I care? Definitely not.

I'll have to watch my back from now on. Worth it, though.

I leave the ATV near a new Buick LaCrosse and swagger across the lot. When I push open the glass door, Floyd's talking to a customer beside a red Malibu. The showroom is smooth and glossy, the floor gleaming, the cars untouched by rain or salt or dirt.

I lean against the door frame, hip cocked, thumbs in my pockets, wait until Floyd notices me, and drawl, "Fancy meeting you here."

His smile goes tight. "What do you want?"

"Just checking your sales pitch."

"Excuse me," he says to the customer, baring his teeth in another smile. "I'll be right back."

See? See what he's really like?

Adrenaline highs are edgier than endorphin highs. I don't

move a muscle. Floyd shoves his face into mine. Lowering his voice, he says, "Get out of here."

"Careful," I say. "You wouldn't want your boss to see the real you. Father and son—I mean, it's kind of touching, isn't it? How about a nice hug?"

For a minute I think he's going to plough me regardless of the consequences. From heel to toe, the soles of my feet connect with the floor; inwardly I rehearse the first block.

"I'll deal with you tonight," he says, his eyes like ice chips. "Out!"

"Oh, before I forget—Opal asked me to give you these."

I toss him the bundle of envelopes, crumpled from my pocket. He snatches them, turns on his heel, and strides back to the customer, who's gazing at us in a puzzled kind of way.

Taking my time, I push the door open and walk past a row of Cobalts. Bet you 300 of my 330 dollars that the sale goes down the tubes.

AT THE end of the river trail, the first thing I see on Hilchey River Road is the garbage truck. I accelerate across the road as it pulls up beside our bin.

Docker jumps down from the tailgate. "Hey, Brick."

I brake and slide to the ground. "You never phoned."

"Was I supposed to?"

"Don't you want to know why I quit?"

He's standing still as a boulder. "You'll tell me when you're ready."

"I just got the best of Snyder McIsaac. Out behind Sobeys."

"Self-defense?"

"He started it."

Docker strides over to the garbage bin, lifts it like it weighs nothing, and throws the contents into the open back of the truck. "Good for you," he says with as much emotion as if I'm a heap of garbage.

"You don't give a damn!"

Neatly he replaces the bin, lid on, at the edge of our driveway. "Let's face it, Brick, I dragged you into karate. But if you're not ready, you're not ready. My mistake. Your choice."

I say slowly, "*Kumite* takes two people."

His face loosens some. "*Kihon* and *kata*—you can do those on your own."

He gives me an easy salute before he steps back on the tailgate; the truck pulls a U-turn.

So what was that conversation all about?

And why do I feel two inches tall?

10.2 [amethyst: spiritual calm and healing]

AS DOCKER disappears down the road on the back end of the truck, AQ shoots up from nowhere and lodges itself in my throat.

AQ + adrenaline = a brutal mix.

The mix doesn't last long. AQ wins, hands down. Floyd's going to cream me when he gets home. I should take my savings out of the bank and buy a one-way ticket on the first bus to Halifax.

Can't. Can't leave Cassie.

Cassie ... I'm supposed to be protecting her, keeping her out of harm's way. For *harm* read *Floyd*. What the hell was I thinking, provoking Floyd like that?

The answer's simple. I wasn't thinking. I was high as a kite, high as if I'd snorted some of Snyder's best, riding the high and forgetting all my own rules, like caution, common sense, and keeping a low profile.

What if Floyd flattens me first, then turns on Cassie? Oh man, I'm the biggest screwup on the planet.

I go behind the garage for a while, where I try to concentrate on blocks, punches, and kicks. No conviction in them. No power behind them.

My knuckles hurt where I punched Snyder. When I kicked him, I used my toes instead of the side of my foot, so they hurt too.

I'll deal with you tonight ...

If I'm flat on the floor, I can't protect Cassie.

WHEN OPAL comes downstairs late afternoon to make herself some herbal tea, I say, "I want you to stay down here until Floyd comes home—he's laying for me."

"What did you do?"

"Does it matter? If it gets out of hand, I want you to stop him."

She fills her Japanese teapot with boiling water and puts it on a tray. "Why did you set him off? I've warned you about that, especially when he's so uptight about work."

"The message being that he can do whatever he wants and Cassie and I are supposed to put up with it? I told you, he hits Cassie!"

"I blame your grandfather for all this."

"Thaddeus? He's been dead for years."

She rubs her hands down her skirt. "He wasn't a good father to Floyd."

Bullying gets handed down, is that what she's saying? I wonder what else gets passed along. "Your mother's sister—your aunt—is she the one who brought you up?"

I've never asked her that before.

"Aunt Grace," Opal says. "Whoever named her was having a bad day." She bangs her pottery mug on the tray. "Once Floyd's home, I'll keep an ear open."

I watch her leave the kitchen, listen to the stairs creak as she climbs them. Her office door closes with a small click.

Is that what she calls keeping an ear open?

Before you know it, I'm bounding up the stairs and flinging the door wide. "Couldn't you at least stay downstairs? What kind of mother are you?"

"If this is the way you're behaving with Floyd, no wonder you're in trouble!"

"I'm sick to death of being used as a punching bag!"

The words hang in the air. Truest words I ever spoke. Took me long enough to say them.

Her wind chimes jingle gently in the breeze.

"I'm also sick of being punished for crap that's not worth bothering about."

Opal says stiffly, "I'll leave the door open. If I hear you're in trouble, I'll come downstairs."

"Don't put yourself out."

"*Thank you* would be a better response."

"Thank you for being such a fabulous mother?"

She slams her mug down on the table beside a cluster of amethyst crystals; tea splashes over the sharp purple edges. "I've always paid for everything you need and I know you pocket the change. I never once complained. To you or Floyd."

"You don't love me or Cassie. You've never loved either one of us. Why did you bother having us?"

She says flatly, "The first time, I let Floyd talk me into getting pregnant. He wanted a son to carry on the MacAvoy name, don't ask me why. Cassie was an accident."

"He's been hitting me since I was six. Do you even care?"

"You never told me."

"Don't give me that—you've seen him."

"Corporal punishment isn't the worst thing that can happen to you. Anyway, I'm not a maternal woman."

"You call that an answer?" *Corporal punishment* ... she's even starting to sound like Floyd.

"I spoke to him the day after we helped you up the stairs ... told him he had to clean up his act."

"Oh, he sure cleaned it up. Just ask Cassie."

"I'll speak to him about that too. We need to move out of this house, I've been saying it for years."

"If he ever lays a hand on her again, I'll go to Social Services and they'll take her away from here. Imagine the gossip in town ... a psychic healer whose husband beats up his kids."

"That's blackmail!"

"You're damn right it is. Speak to him, Opal."

In the breeze, a crystal hanging in the window snicks against the glass. Ripples of color waver on the opposite wall. I walk out, leaving the door ajar.

Floyd will be home soon. And I'll never call the social worker.

My mouth feels like I'm chewing ashes, while my gut's a lump of ice.

10.3 [self-defense]

DOWNSTAIRS, I detach Cassie from *Treehouse* and send her to her room. "You'll be okay. Opal's home. But keep your door shut."

I'm sick to death of a lot of stuff, including the fear in her eyes. Four years old. It's gotta stop.

Floyd parks the Hummer by the garage at precisely 5:10. He throws his briefcase, tie, and linen jacket on the kitchen table; his shirtsleeves are already rolled up. All set for business. Taking me by the arm, he pushes me against the wall. "I lost the sale. You spooked the customer."

Dead calm in my gut now. Any chance it could be called courage? I doubt it. "No," I say, "*you* spooked him. The mask slipped, Floyd, and I wasn't the only one to see it."

He says, spacing his words, "I'm going to give you a beating you'll never forget."

"Go right ahead. I'll go to the dealership tomorrow, take my shirt off in front of your boss, and tell him what happened."

"You little bastard!"

"I wish I was."

He moves so fast I don't see it coming. Grabbing my elbow, he twists me around so I'm nose to the wall and hooks his arm around my neck. Tightens it. Tightens it some more, pressing against my throat. When I try to shout for help, all that comes out is a feeble groan.

Too feeble for Opal to hear.

Little red spots dance in front of my eyes, blackness swirling behind them. Knees buckling. Mouth open, straining to scream.

Docker ... the sleeper hold.

I tuck my chin in, hard, grip Floyd's arm, and pull down in a desperate burst of strength. My fingers dig into his flesh. As his arm loosens, I kick him in the shin, raking my heel down the bone.

Should be wearing Wendell's boots.

Floyd tries to hook me with his other arm. His nails gouge my skin, pain hot as fire.

Throwing myself back, I knock him off-kilter and I'm free, air rasping into my lungs, the black mist still hovering behind my eyes.

Shrill as a fire bell, the telephone rings.

One ring. Opal calls down the stairs, "The phone's for you, Floyd. It's Pete."

My head hanging down, the blackness slowly vanishing, I gulp mouthfuls of air.

Floyd runs his fingers through his hair and picks up the receiver. "Pete," he says genially, "what's up?"

I make it across the room and take the stairs one by one, hauling on the banister. Once I'm in the bathroom, I lock the door. Three raw welts cross my collarbone, all of them bleeding.

I don't look so hot. Face white, twin red patches high on my cheekbones, like a clown in a circus.

10.4 [self-disclosure]

I CAN'T face the thought of running the next morning, of gasping for oxygen as I chug up the hills. But I do bicep curls, and the whole time I'm counting reps I'm remembering how Docker and Michaela showed me how to get out of the sleeper hold.

Sure, the phone call helped—I should send Pete a thank-you card. But first I should send Docker one.

I should eat crow is what I should do. See if he'd take me back. The Official MacAvoy Punching Bag has had it up to the eyeballs.

I tap on Opal's bedroom door. She's feeling better, so I tell her I'm gone for the morning. Then I promise Cassie I'll have a big surprise for her later on, and gather all the stuff I'll need.

Twenty minutes later I'm unloading a broom, dustpan, bucket, scrub brush, and garbage bags from the ATV, which is parked as far off the river trail as I can manage. After lugging the stuff to the hunting shack, I make a second trip for the lattice I stole from the garage, along with a saw and some nails. Once I'm done cleaning the shack, I won't bring the ATV anymore. No sense leaving a signpost saying Brick Is Here.

You don't want to know about the next three hours. But by noon the cobwebs and raccoon shit are gone; the table, chairs, bunks, and floor have been scrubbed with Mr. Clean; and lattice is nailed over the windows with screening to the inside of it. Rain's going to get in, though, even if raccoons and mosquitoes can't. I bet I could figure out how to put glass in the windows— add glazing to my handyman CV.

I look down at myself. I'm not Mr. Clean. I'm downright dirty. I'm also smiling, a smile I can't seem to get rid of.

I tighten the hinges on the door. Putting on a padlock might be asking for trouble, but I'd sure like to bring a few things of my own here. Dishes. Cushions. Candles. A jug or two of drinking water.

Cassie will like it, I know she will. She needs a hideaway as bad as I do.

I fit a piece of lattice over an open knothole in the inside wall, then bang in a couple of nails.

"Hey, Brick."

The hammer hits my thumb and my heart jumps out of my mouth. I pivot, clutching the hammer like a weapon.

Tully's standing in the doorway. I lower the hammer.

She looks around, taking her time. "You've done a great job— the place was a disaster."

"Get lost!"

"I have to talk to you."

I glance down at her feet. "Jeez, I forgot the welcome mat."

"I saw your ATV by the trail. I've known about this place since spring."

She's wearing another of her loose T-shirts, orange, with SAVE THE PLANET written in white across her chest. As she jams her hands in the pockets of her jeans, I realize she's not as much at ease as she'd like me to think.

Do I care? This is my place. My sanctuary, like medieval churches when the king got on your case. "Take your own advice and go save the planet, Tully. It needs busybodies like you."

"I'm not leaving until I've had my say."

"I've had a bellyful of you and your family!"

She walks closer, leans her palms on the table. "On Sunday when I saw the bruises on Cassie's knees and she wouldn't tell me what happened, I didn't know what to do. I didn't really think you were responsible for hurting her, Brick. Although I did wonder if maybe you'd knocked her down by mistake and warned her not to tell."

"I threaten her with machetes every day of the week."

"Someone was responsible for those bruises. I didn't want it to be you—but I had to ask, Brick. I had to! Because it was Cassie and she's only four years old."

A crow starts yammering in a tree outside the window. "You think the worst of me every chance you get."

"Not anymore, I don't ... I know you take Cassie to the beach and the library, and I saw you protect her from Snyder. It's been driving me crazy, not being able to understand you—the bully and the brother. Two sides, and how was I supposed to put them together?" Her whole body's leaning across the table now. "So before you picked her up on Sunday—before I asked you about the bruises—I took her aside and tried to talk to her."

"You've got no right to — "

"She told me how every evening you read to her before bed, then you kiss her good night. That you cook supper for her and comfort her when she has nightscares. None of this adds up to bullying."

"None of it's any of your business," I say in a choked voice.

"It is when Cassie has big bruises on her knees, and more on her back. Because I saw those too, when she was playing with Caramel."

Black wings swoop past the window and the cawing fades into the distance. "So why didn't you show Rolf?" I say bitterly. "That way you could have set the cops on me."

"I had to talk to you first! I'd done a number on you with Rolf already, and I sure didn't want to do it again. When I asked you about the bruises, you looked so ... defeated. As if you couldn't deal with one more thing."

The veins on Tully's arms are the same blue as her ankles. I jerk my eyes away. "Cassie fell off the couch. Hit her back on the corner of the coffee table and landed on her knees."

"If that's all it was, why wouldn't she tell me?"

"She's shy." Even I can hear that's not much of a response.

Tully says, "You're into protecting Cassie. You're doing your best to be a good brother, that's what I've decided."

"Until you change your mind." *C'mon, Brick, you can do anger better than that.*

"You love each other."

Well, duh. Although what I feel for Cassie is a lot more complicated than love. Why do girls always have to drag love in, anyway?

"Rolf," Tully says, "now there's a man who's into protection with a capital *P*. Mom, me, the baby, Caramel, Cassie, Glenn—you name it. When I told him about you and Glenn, I knew he'd come on strong, that he'd turf you out the door. I was too angry to care. But then he had to go to work, and I was left home to stew." She grimaces. "After he talked to Mom and they both agreed they didn't want you at our place, I argued with them. Sort of. But another thing about Rolf is he can be real stubborn. You being a bully—that did it."

"I noticed."

She scuffs the bare floorboards with her sneaker. "I went along with Rolf—Brick-the-bully, who everybody hates. I still hate what you did to Glenn. But I've had time to think. You see, I want a new bike, a Kona, even if it's only the basic model ... so I'm saving every penny I can lay my hands on. Ever since you started mowing Della's lawn, I've been mad at you, which made it easier to side with Rolf. The truth is, you got to Della first. I was mad at myself and took it out on you. I shouldn't have and I'm sorry."

Her eyes look greener inside the shack. Green. Generous. Honest.

"I—okay," I say.

"How did you get those scrapes?"

I wore my oldest T-shirt this morning, the neck stretched way out of shape. "Sharp branches in the woods."

She stands straight. "If you don't want to tell me, say so. But don't lie."

"I can't tell you!"

Now she's chewing on her lip. Taking a deep breath, she says, "If I had to guess, I'd say your dad."

I stare at her blankly. She's only guessing. She doesn't really know.

But my heart's pounding as if Floyd is about to march through the doorway of the shack and punch the living daylights out of me. "You're out of your mind," I mutter.

"When I asked Cassie about him, she looked frightened. Much too frightened for a simple question about her father."

"I already told you, she's shy."

"I talked to Glenn yesterday," Tully says. "You didn't lay a hand on him at the bridge yesterday when you were running. And he told me how you saved Igor."

"Yeah, well ..."

All the light from the two little windows seems to have aimed straight for her hair. She runs her fingers over the grain in the table and takes another deep breath. "My biological father—his name was Buddy—he used to beat my mom."

The river whispers through the trees. A squirrel scrabbles across the roof. I'd better put mesh over the chimney to keep them out. Bats, too.

Say something, Brick.

"I remember her screaming. I remember bruises and black eyes and her making excuses because she loved him." Tully's eyes are bright with tears. "Then he turned on me and that was it. She found the courage to leave him even though she had no money and no job ... I was a only couple of months older than Cassie."

I walk around the table, banging my hip on one corner, hesitate, then rest a hand on her shoulder. Ready to snatch it back if she objects, I say, "I'm sorry."

How lame is that.

She leans on my chest, closing her eyes. I feel dampness. Tears. Tully Langille's tears, soaking through my filthy T-shirt. Clumsily I put my arms around her.

I've come across the word *intimacy*, of course I have. Figured it bypassed me and likely always would—although sometimes I've wondered if my first kiss would give me a handle on it. But right now, Tully leaning on me—trusting me with her secret— puts a whole new slant on it.

All of a sudden, AQ hits the roof of the shack.

We stand like this for a long time. Then she says, so quietly I have to strain to hear her, "Buddy used to swing me way up to the ceiling and pretend he was going to drop me—I've been scared of heights ever since. He was a bully. Mean all the way through."

Nothing I can say that'll fix it. Nothing at all.

"That's why I couldn't figure you out," Tully says. "You were a bully, but you were decent, too ... Rolf knows about Buddy. That's why he reacted so strongly when he found out about you."

"Floyd," I say. "Floyd was angry at Cassie, so he hit her. Then he picked her up and started shaking her. When he dropped her, she hit her back on the coffee table and banged her knees on the floor."

Tully lifts her head so she can look at me. "He beats you, doesn't he?"

"Yeah ... he beats me."

She shivers. "Can't your mom stop him?"

"She did once. A month or so ago."

"Your face, when you had the black eye and all those bruises—was it really Snyder and his gang?"

"No." Now I'm chewing my lip. "Apart from Opal and Cassie, you're the only person who knows about Floyd. Docker might have guessed ... I'm not sure."

"What's Docker got to do with it?"

"For a while I was taking karate lessons from him."

"Self-defense," she says slowly.

"That was the general idea." I step away from her, letting my arms fall to my sides. "Tully, you won't tell anyone about Floyd. Promise?"

"No! That's the whole problem—no one ever says anything."

"I only found out a week ago that Floyd hits Cassie. I was so frigging blind. Ignored all the signals."

"You have to go to the authorities."

"I can't. They'll take Cassie away—put her in a foster home. I'm her big brother, the guy who looks after her. She needs me. She'd miss me, I know she would."

"They'd put you in the same home," she says, sounding doubtful.

"I dunno how it works and I'm scared to find out. I mean, lots of people would want a cute little kid like Cassie. But a semi-reformed bully? I'm no bargain."

"So what are you going to do?"

"I'm too young to take off with her. I'd have to be at least sixteen, and even then I'm not sure I'd get away with it. All I can do is go back to karate, if Docker will have me. I should never have quit. But if I can beat Floyd at his own game, then —"

"That's guy-talk," Tully snaps. "Solve violence with violence."

"It's the only language he understands. I've got to get his attention so he'll stop knocking us around—me and Cassie. Somehow I have to make him respect me, make him understand that I'll turn him in if I have to." AQ zooms up the chimney and out of sight. "I'm not a total idiot. If things get too rough, I'll take Cassie and run."

"If you can."

"Yesterday I held off Snyder McIsaac behind Shoppers. Just me and him, and I came out on top. I gotta do this, Tully. All my life I've felt like a coward—why else do you think I pick on kids smaller than me? If I put the cops onto Floyd now, I'll always be afraid of him."

She sighs, a sigh that comes all the way from her toes. "If I see the smallest bruise on you or Cassie, I'm telling Rolf."

"I wish you'd try and understand where I'm coming from!"

"I do understand—you don't have many choices and they all suck. Brick, if you're in trouble, night or day, our place is just up the road."

"Right. Like Rolf would agree to that."

"If you were in danger? Of course he would."

I run my fingers over the stubble on my head. "I guess he would ... He's a solid sort of guy."

"He's the best. When I get the chance, I'll talk to him about you and—"

"I don't want you to! What if it comes out about Floyd?"

"You've got to trust me," she says.

I look at her in silence. The truth's becoming addictive. "I don't know if I can. Never learned how. Not just you. Anyone."

A breeze wafts through the new lattice. It's as though Floyd's standing between us, keeping us apart.

"You have to start somewhere," she says.

"Easy to say."

She wrinkles her nose. "You know what? Your T-shirt's gross."

"In the fall—after school starts—maybe you and I could go to Tim Hortons, have a coffee."

Did I actually say that?

Her whole face breaks into a smile. "Maybe we could."

I want to kiss her so bad I can taste it. But there are cobwebs in my hair, dirt under my nails, and my T-shirt is beyond gross. Plus I've never figured out which side of the girl's nose you put your nose. "I better clean up in the river."

"I'll carry the bucket if you want to bring the other stuff."

Once we've piled everything outside the shack, I close the door and lean a rock against it. We dump the contents of the bucket under a tree. At the river, I splash water over my face and hands, then wipe them on the hem of the T-shirt.

Tully laughs. "The shack's cleaner than you. You'll wash your face before our date, right?"

A date. With Tully Langille. Me, Brick MacAvoy.

"Are we friends?" The words hang in the air. Too late to snatch them back.

She sobers. "We're heading in that direction."

"Dumb question."

"Buddy used to call me the dumbest kid on the block."

"*You?* Was he crazy?"

"Could be." She shivers again, even though it's hot on the riverbank. "My mom is my hero."

Then Tully gets her bike, which is leaning against my ATV, and we go our separate ways.

11.1 [self-respect]

THAT AFTERNOON Cassie and I walk the river trail to the hunting shack.

Cassie likes the shack.

Rover likes the shack too.

Cassie wants to sleep here.

Not just tonight, every night.

On a scale of one to ten, the tantrum is a four.

I produce the picnic she didn't know I'd made.

We eat peanut butter sandwiches and chocolate chip cookies and drink apple juice, both of us sitting at the table. I brought an old cushion for her to sit on, and a plastic Sesame Street table-cloth. The place is starting to look like home.

"It's our secret place, Cassie," I say. "Tully knows about it—so it's just the three of us."

"It's a nice secret," she says, smiling at me, her chin smeared with raspberry jelly.

Normal. That's all I want. Normal.

EIGHT O'CLOCK. Cassie's already asleep. I close my bedroom door and walk downstairs, past Floyd and the NASCAR races, past Opal, who's sorting a big box of polished stones, through the kitchen and out the door, grabbing my hoodie off the hook on the way.

Easy. So easy it blows my mind.

I jog to the road and turn right.

Docker's not home, no GM pickup in the driveway, no lights on in the house. I don't have a clue what I'm going to say to him. I settle myself on the step to compose my speech.

The mosquitoes discover me. I zip up my hood, walk around, jog up and down the driveway, practice blocks and strikes.

Floyd goes to bed early; once he realizes I'm still out, odds are he'll lock the door. I have my own key, but a pissed-off Floyd I don't need. I'll give Docker until nine o'clock.

It's getting dark earlier now that we're partway into August. I practice locating the mosquitoes by their whining then whacking them. I sit down again, lean against the side door, and drift off.

Gravel crunching, slam of a door. A light shining in my eyes. I blink, throwing my arms in front of my face.

"Hey, Brick," Docker says.

"What's the time?" I say in a panic.

"Quarter to ten."

I should have been home half an hour ago. I pull myself

upright. "Will you let me come back to karate?"

So much for the fancy speech.

He says, "Come inside."

His kitchen is neat and tidy, curtains over the sink, dishes done. "Want a coffee?" he says, turning his back as he pours himself one from the pot on the stove and puts the mug in the microwave to nuke it.

"No, thanks."

A colored photo is stuck to the refrigerator door. I squint at it, resisting the urge to step closer. Docker, no gray in his hair, a blond woman snuggled into him, and a little girl with blond curls, all three laughing like happiness comes easy.

Docker lives alone. This has a bad feel to it. I remember his face when he took Cassie's hand.

"Ginger ale?" he says, glancing at me as the microwave beeps. "Or diet Coke?"

"I shouldn't have quit the dojo—I'm sorry. I didn't even have the guts to tell you face-to-face."

He takes a sip of coffee. "Why did you quit?"

Because I got a life sentence of twelve years. "I can't tell you."

"Why do you want to come back?"

"To learn more blocks, better footwork. Get faster."

"Why?"

He's punching, I'm blocking. No point saying, *So I can beat the crap out of Floyd.* "I handled Snyder. But if his three buddies had been there, I'd have been toast."

"It'll be a while before you can take on four guys bigger than you," he says dryly. "Is that the only reason?"

I stare out the window. "The last two or three weeks—it's like I can do something that makes a difference. Like I feel kind of okay about myself. Every now and then."

"Can you tell me why, Brick?"

My arms are hanging at my sides. "I dunno—it's so freaking complicated. It's like my body's *mine*. What kind of sense does that make?"

If *responsibility* is the heaviest word in the dictionary, *hope* is the scariest.

"Let's say you come back to the dojo. We'll meet three times a week until mid-September. Then I'll expect you to enroll in the beginners' class, which will have kids younger than you as well as adults. There's a charge for lessons, and you'll have to order a *gi*."

I'll pay for it with the lawn money. "Okay."

He gulps more coffee. "Because you'll know more than the others in the class, I'll expect you to help out. The test for white belt is three months after enrolment, so it's a real commitment. You'd better think about it."

"I don't need to."

"Self-defense only."

"I know." With Floyd, it's a non-issue. Same for Snyder and his crew.

He pulls a calendar out of a drawer and we decide on Monday, Wednesday, and Friday every week. But when he starts asking questions about running and weights, I interrupt. "It's late. I gotta go home. Thanks a lot for taking me back, Docker."

"Want me to drive you?"

"No, that's okay."

I hurry out the door and jog home fast. I'll run tomorrow, first thing. Get new weights at the dojo.

Lights are on upstairs, but the downstairs is dark and the door's locked. I turn the key, creep inside, and cross the kitchen. The stairs creak. Floyd comes out of his bedroom, closing the door behind him. He's wearing a white tank top and boxers. Flab has started to settle around his waist. First time I've noticed.

"Where have you been?" he says.

You ever seen the eyes on a dead fish?

"I was out for a walk. Needed to think about some stuff."

"Were you with a girl?"

"I wish." I try a man-to-man grin. Abandon it when he doesn't respond. Heart going *whomp-whomp-whomp*.

"What sort of stuff?"

"School stuff. We have some options next year, so I'm trying to decide whether to take geography or physics. For physics I'd need another math course. That kind of thing."

"When you leave the house at night, you tell me where you're going and how long you'll be."

"Yessir."

His hand snakes out, cracks me on the side of the head. Pain, fierce and fast as a flash of lightning. I grunt, knocked off balance. But as my left arm sweeps across my body, *gedan barai*, I halt it, mid-move. Karate's my secret. I can't tip him off, not until I'm ready.

From their bedroom, Opal calls irritably, "Floyd, come back to bed."

He steps nearer, thrusting his face into mine. "I don't like the way you're behaving these days. I think it's time to teach you a lesson."

I step backward and it's not into back stance. "Sorry, sorry," I gabble, "I won't do it again."

Won't do what?

"Yes," he says, "that's what you need. Time and place? You'll find out."

He turns his back. The bedroom door shuts behind him.

11.2 [guerrilla warfare]

THE NEXT morning, I'm headed for the bathroom thinking Floyd's already left for work. He comes out of his bedroom, crowds me against the wall, and steps on my bare foot with his shoe. Leans all his weight on it.

I suck in my breath. It feels like every bone in my foot is about to crack.

I won't be able to run.

He steps back, laughs. "Sorry," he says, "didn't see you standing there."

I could've brought my arms up and shoved him in the chest. Next time, I will.

A few minutes later, I go downstairs to make Cassie's breakfast. The kettle's boiling for Opal's chamomile tea. Floyd lifts it off the stove and pours water into her Japanese teapot. Before I realize what he's up to, he dumps the rest of the water in the sink near where I'm standing. Scalding water splashes my hand.

"You should be more careful around boiling water," he says with that empty smile of his. "Didn't your parents teach you anything?"

So for my first lesson back at the dojo, I have three scabs on my collarbone, blisters on the back of my hand, and bruises on the top of my foot. Docker takes all this in. He looks at me. I look at him. Neither of us says anything. We begin warming up.

Before I leave, we work out a training schedule:

Three days a week:	jog to warm up, then run. Jog to cool down. Stretch. Practice all stances, blocks, kicks, punches, and the moves of *Heian Shodan*, the *kata* Docker is teaching me. He's also added a side-thrust kick and five-step sparring, head and stomach level, along with more self-defense moves using elbows and knees.
Remaining three days:	warm-up, jog, and skip on the spot. Do weights and stretch. Practice karate. Practice knee and elbow strikes.
Three times a week:	lessons at the dojo, ninety minutes long. By the end of

them, I won't be able to stand
up, let alone focus.

In between, of course, I have to mow Della's grass,
look after Cassie, and stay out of Floyd's way.

PROBLEM IS, I can't. Stay out of his way, I mean. He won't
let me. The day after my first lesson, he starts a mock boxing
match with me in the living room in front of Opal and Cassie. Although he's laughing and joking, his punches are mean, the place-
ment ugly. I don't defend myself. It's too soon.

Cassie is cowering in her chair, her eyes wide with terror. I
duck behind the armchair. "I give up," I say, raising my hands,
chest exposed. "You win."

"I always win, kiddo," he says and draws back his fist again.

"Opal, tell him I surrender."

She says, "Stop it, Floyd. It's not funny."

She's frowning at him. He stops. I take Cassie by the hand
and we go upstairs.

Sometime in the middle of the night, I wake with a start.
Rain's pounding on the roof like the entire Canadian army is on
the march. My bedroom door is open. I always shut the door
before I go to bed. Always.

The wind's up. Branches scrabble against the windowpane. I
lie still, gazing into the darkness.

NEXT MORNING Floyd orders me to cut the grass. "But it rained last night," I say.

"Your point is?"

"It's supposed to dry up today. I'll cut it tomorrow."

He bounces on the balls of his feet. "*You* obey *me*—that's the correct order of the pronouns. Cut the grass today."

I want to smash my fist into the smirk on his face. Cutting wet grass is a pain in the ass. He knows this. So do I. I go outside, haul the mower out of the garage, and fill the tank with gas. By the time I'm done, I'm soaked in sweat.

After I shower, I make sandwiches and load my backpack with juice packs and a couple of books. Cassie stuffs Theodore Tugboat, her farm animals, and Rover in her pink carryall, Rover's head flopping over the edge so he can see where we're going. His white stripe is a grimy gray.

Separating him and Cassie long enough to put him through the washer and dryer requires courage, stamina, and two deaf ears.

We walk along the river trail to the shack. After we float Theodore in the river, we sit at the table (same Sesame Street tablecloth plus a red candle on a saucer) and munch egg salad sandwiches and Oreos.

I've brought two more pillows from the linen cupboard. We lie on the bunk while I read to her from *Thidwick, The Big-Hearted Moose*. We doze off.

Anyone watching would think, *How cute ... big brother taking time from his busy life to be with his little sister.*

The next twelve years of his busy life.

While Cassie and I are eating supper, Floyd walks through

the kitchen and gives her hair a playful tug. She squeals in pain.

My muscles tense, all set to eject me from the chair and into his face. Gripping the edge of the chair, I sit still. Repeat three times after me: *I'm not ready. I'm not ready. I'm not ready.*

WHEN I wake up the next morning, the books that were on my bureau when I went to bed are lying on the floor. Don't get me wrong, I'm not worried he's edging toward sexual abuse like some of the parents in the anxiety book. Opal is Floyd's drug of choice. Cat toying with baby robin, that's the name of his game.

And it's working. I'm not sleeping so well the last few nights. Hate the thought of him creeping into my room, watching me, messing with my stuff in the middle of the night. He never used to come in my room, so he's breaking his own rules. If he'll break this rule, which others will he bend out of shape?

AQ? Well, you don't have to be very smart to plot that on the graph. But here's another variable. RQ. Rage Quotient.

Long, humid August days with RQ and AQ rising in tandem. AQ cold. RQ hot. AQ's message: don't do anything. RQ's? Go for the throat.

I'VE JUST had my third lesson with Docker, and I'm carrying Cassie's plate to the table, goulash made with ground beef and stewed tomatoes—her next favorite after chicken fingers. Floyd is carrying a bowl of Tostitos into the living room, Tostitos and Ultimate Fighting being his favorites. He sticks out his foot and trips me. The plate and the goulash go flying, and I bang my face on the edge of the table.

"My apologies," he says.

Cassie's face crumples; she's shaking like a leaf in the wind. Rage throbs in my chest.

Not here. Not now. Not yet.

I get a roll of paper towel, clean up the mess, and refill Cassie's plate. We eat upstairs under her tent.

I don't sleep well, and by morning my cheek sports a crooked blue bruise. Can't go near Tully until it fades or she'll bicycle straight to the RCMP.

THAT AFTERNOON, as Cassie and I are leaving the hunting shack, we hear music coming through the trees. Flute music.

Her eyes go huge. She probably thinks it's Peter Pan or the Pied Piper. We follow the sound and find Glenn perched on a rock beside the river playing this—yep—really neat tune. Cassie walks right up to him. "You own Igor."

He takes his mouth from the flute. "Igor owns me."

"Can you play 'Twinkle, Twinkle, Little Star?'"

He obliges, jazzing it up some. Then he slips into the Sesame Street theme, her clapping her hands to the beat.

I say, "I didn't know you came down here to play your flute."

"I never used to, in case it ended up in the river. Accidentally."

Ouch. Direct hit. So does he feel safe now? "I like the tune you were playing." It was haunting, melancholy, like a slow-moving stream.

"'Komorebi' ... Sunlight Shining through the Trees," he says.

"That's Japanese!"

"Popularized by James Galway. If I could play the flute like him, I'd be one happy dude."

Glenn already is a happy dude. "Practice helps," I say, as if I know what I'm talking about.

"According to my dad, 10,000 hours."

I do the math in my head. 10,000 hours ÷ 12 years = 833 hours/year. Or approximately 2 hours/day. Is that enough to become a 10th Dan black belt?

Will Glenn ever smile for real around me? Weird how much I'd like that.

Or am I after forgiveness? Forgiveness is considerably more complicated than a smile.

11.3 [Sensei (teacher)]

WHEN I arrive for my next lesson, the dojo is empty. Sometimes Docker gets held up if there's heavy-duty garbage along his route. The old guy in the photo gazes at me—I swear he's not as disapproving as he used to be. I take off my shoes and bow at him.

My guts are on the jitter, my head aches, and my eyes are burning from lack of sleep. The bruise on my cheek is a mix of mauve and yellow. I start to warm up, jogging on the spot, swinging my arms, then doing jumping jacks, knee-raises, punches, and more punches.

If I can't sleep, when will I ever be ready?

Docker comes in wearing his *gi* with its frayed black belt. He's carrying some equipment which he piles on the floor. His eyes flick to the bruise and flick away. "I've already warmed up," he says and bows to me.

Automatically I bow back. He barks a command. "Ready stance, *yoi-dachi!*"

My feet go shoulder-width apart, fists at hip height.

"Left downward block, *gedan barai*. Right reverse punch, *gyaku-zuki*. *Gedan barai*. *Gyaku-zuki*. Rising block, *age-uke*. *Gyaku-zuki*. Outside block, *soto-uke*. *Gyaku-zuki*. *Yoi-dachi.*"

I'm hard-pressed to keep up, even though I've been practicing. He slows down a bit, and we go through it again. Then again, faster.

He picks up two fair-sized pads covered in black vinyl and a couple of inches thick, slipping his hands through the elasticized handles on the back.

"I want you to do a series of stepping punches, *oi-zuki*. So far we've practiced No Contact—stopping the punch just short of the opponent's body. Today I want you to hit me." He positions his arms in front of his chest. "These are shock absorbers, so you can't hurt me. But I need to know how much power you're putting into your punches."

I don't want to do this.

"*Yoi-dachi*," he says.

Every muscle in my body has seized up. I put my feet apart, shake my shoulders, try to sink into readiness.

"Three stepping punches, *kiai* on the third. *Oi-zuki*."

My fist stops short of the black vinyl. I'm shivering.

"*Oi-zuki*."

Same thing. Big fat zero. *You're so dumb, kiddo* ... wonder how you say that in Japanese.

"*Oi-zuki!*"

Doesn't this guy know when to quit? My front foot slaps the floor, I rotate my fist, and maybe he shifted the vinyl nearer, I don't know, but my fist hits it, *thwack*.

I don't stop to think. Knees together. Step. Slap my foot. Rotate my fist. Punch. *Thwack*.

Knees together. Step. Slap. Rotate. Punch. *Thwack*.

We're moving fast the length of the room. He looks calm, focused.

I gotta quit this. Now.

Step. Slap. Rotate. Punch. Power behind my fist. His face unchanged, like nothing's happening.

Step. Punch with all the force I'm capable of. Step. Punch, punch, punch and all I'm hitting is the goddamn vinyl, my whole body behind every stroke—but I can't reach him because he's blocking me.

Fury floods my brain. Breath sobs in my lungs. *I'll kill the bastard, I'll kill him, I can't hang in for twelve years, I'll kill him ...*

Pain judders through my shoulder with each punch. Fists on fire. But I can't stop, nothing will stop me until he's dead. Every beating he ever laid on me, every bruise, every black eye and humiliation power my fists, shrill from brain to knuckle punch-punchpunchpunchpunch.

He won't fall down. The sonofabitch won't fall down.

I lean my weight on him, jabbing him, kicking, kneeing, but I'm slowing down because I hurt all over, and someone's swearing, a string of obscenities in a voice I don't recognize, a voice that's nothing to do with me.

Then this same guy starts sobbing, great gasps heaving from

his gut, rasping up his throat. He slides to the floor in a heap, sounds coming out of him, animal sounds.

A man kneels beside me. I curl around myself, quick, in case he kicks me, wrapping my arms around my head.

A howl bursts out from deep in my belly—a howl into the night from a dog that's lost and hungry.

A howl louder than any *kiai*.

Docker says gently, "Your father beats you. I wondered, that day you had trouble with the green bin. And I've wondered since then. Guess I didn't want to believe a man could inflict that kind of damage on his son."

He knows. Docker knows the truth about Floyd. A wave of relief has me floating off the floor.

Then, like he stuck a pin in me, I crash.

I can't risk losing Cassie. I better deny it—fast. Scrubbing at my face, I lever myself up on one elbow.

Docker pushes a box of Kleenex toward me and watches me blow my nose. He says, "The police—they deal with domestic violence."

I open my mouth, then shut it. There's no point in denial. Not with Docker. "You want to get me killed?" I say, trying to sound like I'm joking and making a half-assed job of it.

"I saw your face that day. It was a mess."

Someone's opened a tap and drained every drop of rage from my body. Into that emptiness, relief floods back, stronger than before. Docker's decent, and in his impassive way, he's tough. Maybe now I won't have to deal with everything on my own.

Two people know. Docker and Tully.

He says, "Where's Cassie when all this is going on?"

"I keep her safe."

He reaches out a hand and pulls me to my feet. I drop his hand fast as I can, swaying on my feet. In a hoarse voice, I say, "Was this a setup? Let's get Brick to lose his cool and see what happens?"

"What we just did with the pads is standard karate practice. It was your response that wasn't standard."

"He'll do me in if he finds out that you know."

"He won't find out," Docker says.

A shudder runs through me. "Wish I could believe you."

"Brick, trust me, he's not going to do you in. Ever. We'll step up the lessons to two hours—the quicker you learn to defend yourself the better—and we'll work harder on strikes. In the meantime, I'll keep my mouth shut. If you get beat up again, though, I'm going to the police."

My knees quiver with the strain of staying upright. The police ... not the police. "You don't understand the first thing about it!"

"So explain."

I grope through the words in my head. "If they find out, they'll take Cassie away ... put her in a foster home. I can't lose Cassie, she's my kid sister."

"You're both under sixteen. They'd put you in the same place."

"Guaranteed?"

He suddenly looks older. Old and tired. "No guarantees of anything, Brick. But I'd go to bat for the two of you, to keep you together."

Gaping at him, I say, "With Social Services, you mean? Or in court?"

"Both."

I scrub at my face again. "Oh."

He smiles at me. "Let's not borrow trouble. For now, you and I have work to do. A lot of work. How's the running? And the weights?"

"You'd put yourself on the line for me and Cassie?"

"That's what I said."

"Why?"

"All men aren't like your father, Brick."

Docker's nothing like Floyd. I can trust him, that's what he's saying.

Another secret bursts out of my mouth. "I like running. I might even get good at it." Then I wait to see if he'll laugh in my face.

"You've got the right build," he says casually. "No excess fat." He glances at the clock on the wall. "We've done enough for today. Saturday at ten?"

My head's whirling, and I'm so tired I can barely stand up. "Can I bring Cassie?"

"Sure. In the meantime, practice everything we've covered so far. And Brick—" He grins at me. "There's plenty of power behind your punches."

11.4 ["The Razor's Edge"]

THAT NIGHT I shove my chair under the door handle and sleep the night through. I surface with a tactic staring me in the face. Beat Floyd on stamina.

Flab around his gut from too many Tostitos and too much TV. His idea of Ultimate Fighting is to wallop his kids. The only exercise he gets is strolling around the lot at the dealership. Sure, he can still flick a mean punch. But how many in a row, and for how long?

I go for my run because Floyd's working, even though it's Saturday. It's painful for the first few minutes until I loosen up the soreness from yesterday's slugfest. But gradually I start feeling how easy I breathe and how strong my quads and calves are. Strength and energy: I drink 'em in like Gatorade.

Already I'm on Swamp Road. As I round the sharp turn by

the brook, a deer is browsing on shrubs in the ditch. A doe. Her head jerks up, leaves sticking out of the corner of her mouth. She leaps onto the bank and bounds through the stumps in the clear-cut, white tail flashing. Graceful. Elegant. Wish I could run like that.

Later, I practice karate in the backyard, pushing myself— sometimes dancing around like a boxer, sometimes planting my feet for balance.

Kiai still gets stuck partway up my throat.

Doesn't matter. Yelling isn't going to defeat Floyd.

Defeat Floyd? Defeat *Floyd?* Is that what I'm thinking of doing?

Not a breath of wind, heat gripped by the clearing, the woodpile shimmering. I drop to the ground, head between my knees. I'm outta my mind.

Okay. So not this week. Or next.

First thing you know I'll be back in school. The bus picks me up early, drops me off late. Not much time for running or karate. I'll get out of shape.

Panic streaks along my nerves. I can't do this. I can't.

When Floyd comes home from work, I'm head and shoulders in the mudroom closet, where I'm searching for Cassie's flip-flops. He knocks me sideways and twists my arm behind my back until my shoulder feels like it's coming out of its socket. Has he ever googled *dislocation?*

Don't cry, don't give him the satisfaction.

Instead I make these guttural noises—easy enough to do and just enough to keep him happy. When he lets go, my eyes are dry. I do my best to keep any hint of victory from showing.

He says, "That was just a warm-up. There's more to come. I'll keep you posted." Lines in his face I haven't noticed before—deep lines, like gouges.

An insight zings through my brain. He's stepped up the pace the last week or so because he's afraid he's losing control.

Floyd afraid? Better than winning Lotto 6/49.

12.1 [man to man]

SUNDAY AFTERNOON, I phone Marigold to see if I can leave Cassie there the following afternoon while I'm at my lesson.

"I'd love to see her," Marigold says. "It's been a while."

Guess it has. Time goes fast when you're having fun.

The bruise on my cheek has mostly faded. Truth is, it was convenient. I'm scared to see Tully again in case she's changed her mind. About our date. About me.

She's not around when I deliver Cassie.

But when I push open the glass door of the dojo after the lesson, Rolf is standing there.

My heart jolts in my chest. "Is something wrong with Cassie?"

"She's good."

I don't look my best. T-shirt soaked in sweat, wet bandanna

around my forehead. Head ringing with instructions, a big jabber of Japanese and English.

Rolf says, "You got a couple minutes?"

"I have to pick Cassie up from your place, that's all."

"She can stay for supper. Let's go sit down."

"What's up?" I ask.

"I gotta talk to you."

The block hasn't been invented that would work against Rolf Langille; if I take off, he'll just wait for me at his place.

The mall anchored some tables and chairs near three fake fig trees and a fountain they never turn on. I sprawl on one of the chairs. It's plastic. Uncomfortable. Malls have this thing about loitering.

Rolf says, "After I got home from work yesterday, Tully sat me and Marigold down. Said we had to trust her and not ask questions. Said we'd been misjudging you. That you really have quit bullying. That you never bullied Cassie. Never have, never will. That you never touched drugs or had dealings with Snyder and his gang."

He labors on. "Tully—that girl has a good head on her shoulders. Talks a lot of sense, and she's honest as the day is long. So Marigold and me, we hashed it over before we went to bed. The reason we jumped on you so hard was because of Buddy, the guy she used to live with. Tully's father. He broke Marigold's jaw once." His big hands curl into fists. "He'd best stay out of my way, that's all I can say."

"Tully told me about him."

"She did?" Rolf gives me a considering look. "She doesn't talk about him much. She must like you."

I don't know what to say to this, so I don't say anything.

"Snyder and his crew beat you up bad—your face looked like you'd walked into a light pole," Rolf says. "That why Docker's teaching you karate?"

I dig at the plastic table with my fingernail. I wish I had the nerve to tell him about Floyd. But if I do, he'll go straight to the cops. "Docker's great," I say.

"Your dad no help? He used to box, didn't he?"

"Not anymore."

"I'm sorry I came down on you so hard, Brick. Real sorry. So's Marigold—but she'll tell you that herself. And if there's anything I can do to help, you just let me know ... I could teach you a trick or two about down-and-dirty fighting."

Fourteen-year-old guys don't cry in public. I dig my nails into my palm instead of the table.

"We want you to know you're welcome at our place anytime. Day or night." He tugs his ear. "Cassie will like it when the baby arrives."

An image whips through my brain of Cassie living with Marigold and Rolf ... safe, happy, loved. How good would that be?

It'll never happen. Still, we have another place to go and decent people to go to.

Finally, I look up. When I do, Rolf smiles at me. A real smile, eyes and all.

He says gruffly, "I gotta job for you if you're interested. Marigold and me bought a bunch of secondhand furniture at an auction. It all needs refinishing. Finicky work, takes time and patience. Can't pay much, but I can teach you a bit about wood-working as we go."

I clear my throat. "It's a deal."

He reaches across the table with his right hand. Scars on his knuckles, coarse hair on the back of his hand. Funny how it grows there and not on top of his head. We shake hands; he's got a grip like a lumberjack. He says, "You need a drive?"

"The ATV is parked out back."

"See you at the house, then." He gives me another of those smiles. "Barbecued spareribs and Caesar salad. Marigold makes the best Caesar from Yarmouth to Canso."

After we walk out of the mall together, he waits until the ATV roars into action before he heads for his truck.

The river trail jounces me along. I've been alone with the whole Floyd thing for so long that it feels weird to have allies. Places I could go for help. People who would believe me. My gut tells me Rolf and Marigold would, the same way Tully and Docker did.

What will happen if Floyd finds out our dirty laundry is sloshing around at the Laundromat on Main Street?

```
Assignment:  plot the number of people who know
             about Floyd on the horizontal axis,
             DQ (Danger Quotient) on the vertical
             axis.
```

Easy assignment, huh?

12.2 [Tully]

TULLY IS perched on the doorstep when I arrive. Under the trees, taking my time, I shift to neutral, put the hand brake on, turn off the ignition, swing my leg over the seat, and shove the key in my pocket. Then I walk across the grass.

"Hi," I say.

"Hi." Her eyes are as turbulent as the river in spring ... and I gotta stop the Wordsworth crap.

She doesn't say anything else. I can't think of anything else to say. The crickets chirrup in the grass.

Then Cassie bursts out the door. "Guess what, Brick? Caramel can roll over and play dead."

We all go indoors. The spareribs taste great, and so does the salad. Marigold takes me aside, apologizes, and kisses me on the cheek.

She looks tired, her belly dragging her down in the heat. While I load the dishwasher and Tully hand washes the barbecue tools, Rolf cleans the barbecue. Tully hasn't spoken to me since we came inside. As water swirls down the sink, I make a stab at courage. "Tully, can we go outside for a minute?"

"Guess so."

We leave Cassie lying on the carpet nose-to-nose with Caramel and stand in the shade by the fire pit. AQ is cruising the treetops. She says, talking fast, "The baby robins have learned to fly. Both of them."

I run my fingers over my hair. Past time I went back to the barber. "Thanks for talking to your parents."

"Since the day at the hunting shack, has your father beaten you?"

The lie starts tripping off my tongue. "Nah, he—" Then I stop. "He's been ... difficult."

"There's a yellow smudge on your cheekbone. Looks like an old bruise."

"He tripped me."

"Is that why you've been avoiding me? It's nearly two weeks!"

So her temper's up. Although it's not just temper. She's nervous. She was never nervous of me when I was in bully mode.

"Do you still want to go to Tim Hortons?" I say.

"Why wouldn't I?"

"Well ... because I'm a jerk?"

"I was worried about you!"

AQ has me by the throat. "I was afraid you'd be sorry you made a date with me. And sorrier for telling me about Buddy."

"No and no. But it was a big deal talking about Buddy. Then you just walked away—and stayed away—as though nothing happened."

"I'm sorry." I really am. Another insight zaps me between the eyes. What I do matters to Tully.

She bends down to pick a dandelion and begins shredding the petals. "Okay," she says.

"Rolf thinks the world of you. Told me so."

Her hands grow still. "I love my dad."

"You're lucky. I mean, I know it was hard, early on, but now you're safe. You and your mom."

"You will be too," she says fiercely.

"Docker knows about Floyd."

"Docker would lay charges if anything happened."

I pick a dandelion too. The broken ends of the stem curl up. "I wanted to tell Rolf the truth. But I chickened out."

"You'll tell him. Or Mom. Sooner or later."

I look at her helplessly. "I'm scared to death of Floyd."

"You'd be a fool not to be."

"Dunno if I can fight him. I'm such a coward, Tully."

"Would you have called my mom a coward when Buddy was six feet tall, built like a wrestler, and mean to the core?"

"Um ... no."

"You're not a coward to be scared of Floyd. You're smart."

"You really mean that?"

"How old were you when he started hitting you?" she says.

"Six."

"Of course I mean it!"

I shuffle my feet in the grass. "I thought the world would come to an end if I ever talked about Floyd."

"Guess what? The garage is still standing, the house is still Sunshine Yellow, and I bet Caramel and Cassie are snoring on the kitchen floor."

I lean forward and kiss her on the cheek. So quick I barely feel her skin—and then it's over.

She says, "Let's not wait for school to start before we go to Tim Hortons. We could meet in town some day. I landed another babysitting job, with tourists staying at Seaview Cottages."

"Yeah," I say, my smile just about splitting my face in two, "let's do that. And I plan on speaking to Della about the lawn. I'll ask her if she's okay with you doing it."

"We could divide it up. You one week, me the next." Then she reaches up, kisses me on the mouth, and steps back. "We better go in," she says.

Her nose and my nose—it worked just fine.

12.3 [Hockey Night in Hilchey Bay]

WHEN CASSIE and I go home, Opal and Floyd are both in the living room. Floyd says, "Where have you been?"

"We took a picnic by the river."

"Cassie, where were you?"

She shrinks back. Says nothing.

"You'll both eat supper at home from now on."

Keep your cool. It's too soon to provoke him. "Yes, sir."

His lips thin. "I registered you for hockey today."

"No."

Silence thick enough to serve as porridge for breakfast. "What do you mean, *no*? You're in Midget this year."

I stand tall; the muscles in my legs tighten. "I'm not playing hockey this winter."

262 ● Jill MacLean

"You'll do as I say."

"I'm into running. And weights."

"Good. Perhaps your hockey will improve."

"I hate hockey! I have for years."

"You think I care?"

"I know you don't."

Opal interrupts. "Cassie, it's past your bedtime. Go upstairs and clean your teeth. Brick, you'll do as your father says."

"I'm not playing hockey. What's he going to do—tape my mouth shut and drag me out on the ice?"

Right now, RQ feels as cold as ice. Bizarre. "In case you hadn't noticed, Opal, I'm not a kid anymore. Next time he hits me, I'm going to report him to the cops."

"We'll see about that," Floyd says.

I brace myself, but he doesn't make a move, just stares at me like he's never seen me before.

"I'm going upstairs," I say. "Good night."

Turning my back on him feels like teetering, blindfolded, on the edge of a cliff with a firing squad behind me.

Nothing happens.

I walk up the stairs, go into my room, and close the door. For a long time I lie awake, thinking. Floyd, Docker, Rolf, Mr. Semple. Which one do I want to be like when I grow up? Or will I turn into Floyd regardless?

12.4 ["If You Want Blood (You've Got It)"]

TWO DAYS later, I'm home by myself for once. Opal has taken Cassie into town to register her at Happy Whale Daycare because the unpaid babysitter—me—will soon be in school.

Floyd's biding his time. AQ is astronomical.

It's the hottest day so far this summer, temperature in the mid-thirties, humidity like wading upriver. I go through my routine anyway then turn on the TV, just because I can.

A vehicle drives up to the house. The Hummer. Floyd never comes home for lunch.

I stand back from the kitchen windows and watch. His shirt-sleeves are rolled up. No tie. He marches to the backyard and starts tugging logs from the woodpile, tossing them on the grass. Has he gone out of his mind?

Serious question.

Has he?

I decide I'd better find out.

He hears me coming. Another log thumps to the grass. He says, "I want this woodpile re-stacked into a Shaker round. I'll be back in two hours to check on you."

"In this heat? Are you crazy?"

"Do what I say!"

Remember playing hide-and-seek? *Ready or not, here I come ...*

"No, sir."

"Do it," he says, stepping closer.

His voice shivers along my nerves. "Make me."

His fist is a blur. Straight to the gut and no time to block. I trip over a log, fall backward, and crash into the woodpile. Pain front and back. Gulping air, I watch him move in for the attack. Won't be a knock-out blow—he wants to enjoy this.

At the last second, I dodge sideways so his next blow glances off my ribs. Gives me time to get my feet under me. *Don't forget to breathe ... and focus, man, focus.*

He aims for my jaw. I do a rising block and it works, by God it works. As he snarls like a chained dog, I try to keep my head. We're close enough that I jab him hard in the chest with my elbow.

His breath hisses through his teeth. He punches me in the belly, a ferocious punch that comes from nowhere. My chin snaps forward.

Like I'm a machine, my right elbow's back. Left downward block, his fist grazing my arm.

Gotta move away from the woodpile. Wishing I was barefoot, risking a glance at the ground so I don't fall over another log, I bounce away from him. "Come on, Floyd, come and get me."

Quicker than I expected, he's after me. Sun blazing down on us—I better be careful it's not in my eyes. I drop low, another rising block then a reverse punch, knuckles to flesh, that sound that's been part of my life for years.

Not enough power. Not nearly enough. Remember what Docker said—elbows and knees.

Floyd's temper is getting the better of him. I feint, dance out of his reach, land a side-kick to his knee that he never saw coming. But he does the same dance, fists coming at me so fast I lose it. Two hard thuds, pain stabbing my chest, sweat dripping down my forehead, blinding me.

"Got you, kiddo! I'm going to give you a thrashing you'll never forget."

Terror immobilizes me. Fist to the solar plexus. I double over, trip over another log and I'm down. Feet coming at me, his polished, hard-soled shoe poised to kick. I grab his ankle and twist, throwing my weight behind it, and down he goes.

I'm up, swipe the sweat from my eyes. As he rolls over and pushes himself upright, his face is bright red. All I have do is hang in, keep him moving.

Keep the sun in *his* eyes.

I prance away, elbow back, fist folded. Because he's angry and not thinking straight, he follows, aiming for my stomach again. Knife-hand block, then I snap out another punch. As my

fist drives into his chest, a noise comes all the way from my gut.
Kiai.

He staggers. I skip to the side and kick him in the shin. Snap
my foot back, watch him stagger some more.

Front stance, move in, elbow-strike to his chin, another to
his ribs, stomp on his foot, and, *kiai.* Sweat's pouring down his
forehead. What'll I do if he has a heart attack?

Fury and frustration bite into his face. I risk looking into his
eyes. Mistake. Murder, pure and simple.

I spring back again, away from the shade, my whole body
on high alert. Move in so he slashes at me. Block, dance back,
dance away.

And I keep this up. Relentless. Ruthless. The point of my
elbow spears his Adam's apple. Side of my foot to his kneecap.
Knees, elbows, kicks, again and again, and always on the move.

"Come on, Floyd—you're not going to let your stupid son
beat you at your own game. Hit me, Floyd. Hit me."

He bellows in rage, charges me—but I'm not there, I'm somewhere else, knees bent, body low, adrenaline ripping through my
veins.

"What's up, Floyd? Can't take the heat? That's a pun, did you
get it?"

He's panting like a dog, like Wilbur used to pant when I was
fetching him water. Before Floyd shot him.

Floyd's shirt is glued to his chest. I taunt him, play with him
some more—his game of cat and baby bird except now I'm the
cat and he's the bird, and I'm loving every minute of it.

Seek perfection of character ... Docker wouldn't be loving this.

For a split second, I falter. Floyd lurches toward me, his chest unguarded, open.

I go cold. *Finish it, Brick.*

Two good punches would knock him flat. Two punches, each fueled by a lifetime of humiliation.

I bounce sideways. He follows me—his eyes manic, glued to mine. I retreat, feigning fear. He makes this sound, roar of a crippled lion, doesn't see the two logs until his toe stubs them. He flails at the air, topples. Thud of his knees on the hard ground. Rasp of his breath.

He tries to push himself up on his elbows. Collapses.

I stand over him, sweat dripping down my face. "Maybe I'm not so dumb after all, Floyd. Maybe I'm a hell of a lot smarter than you."

He's huddled over, groaning. I turn away, take four or five steps toward the trees, and heave up my breakfast. Breakfast, supper last night, every meal I ever ate, until my throat feels raw. I did it. I beat him at his own game.

I retch and spit, scrub my mouth on my T-shirt.

Floyd's still lying on the ground, he's sobbing. I want to run, run faster than I've ever run in my life, and never come back to this heat-soaked clearing, to the knife-edged shadow of an old house.

Words are mixed in with the sobs, incoherent, broken words. "I never locked you in the cellar cupboard. Not once."

Keeping a safe distance between us, because I don't trust this man—I won't ever trust him—I sink down on my haunches. "So?"

"Never beat you with a belt buckle."

Is this about Thaddeus? Do I give a shit?

"I've tried to be a decent father. Tell me—"

"You weren't!"

As he grabs for my hand, I freeze. He's still blubbering. "I hated him, oh God, how I hated him. But I loved him too. I couldn't stop loving him, no matter what he did."

Floyd's nailed it. Hate in one corner, love in the other. Aghast, I look down at him. Hunched over, hugging himself, bawling like a baby—what's there to love?

"You better get up," I say.

"I c-can't."

"You don't want Opal coming home and finding you like this. Let's go indoors, so you can clean up. I'll call Pete and tell him you're sick."

My flesh cringes as I help him to his feet. After I loop his arm over my shoulders, we stagger across the grass to the house. Thaddeus's house.

Grunting, because he's heavy, I lever him into the mudroom. "Opal's right. You need to sell this fricking house. Buy a new one in town."

"He never once told me he loved me," Floyd snivels. "I was his only son."

I ram him against the door frame. "My name's Brickson— remember? I'm your only son."

He gapes at me, tears and sweat coursing down his face.

"Let me get this straight," I say. "Thaddeus used to beat you up, so that makes it okay for you to do the same to me? And to Cassie? Is *that* your sales pitch?"

Another sobs bursts from his chest. His eyes are the same gray as mine.

Will I beat my kids?

"Go upstairs," I say harshly. "Take a shower. You'll have to toss out that shirt—grass stains all over it."

Blood as well. I look down at my knuckles; the skin's scraped and bleeding. If I don't sit down soon, I'm going to faint at his feet.

Floyd reels away from the wall. There are grass stains on his trousers as well.

"I'm sorry," he says. And that's all he says.

What does he want? The big reconciliation scene with me slobbering all over him? I watch him lurch through the kitchen, leaning on the chairs for support. Then I slide down the wall to the floor and rest my head on my knees.

12.5 [rerun]

BY THE time Floyd comes downstairs wearing a fresh shirt, his damp hair combed neatly to his scalp, I've managed to wash my hands and splash water on my face.

I feel like I just ran the Boston Marathon.

He leans against the doorframe, hipshot. It doesn't quite come off. He knows it and so do I.

He says, "Where did you learn to fight like that?"

"Docker Lonergan. He's been teaching me karate."

"So that's where you've been. Picnics by the river—you've been lying to me. Day after day. You and Cassie."

"I'm not lying when I say I won't play hockey."

"It's the only sport in town!"

"Running, weight lifting, and karate—that's what I'm doing this winter." So I'll be faster, stronger, tougher; that's what I'm really saying. He's smart enough to catch on.

"All these years I've paid for your hockey. I'm not paying for karate, kid." He smiles, pleased with that last sentence.

"I don't need your money. Della Barnes is paying me for yard work, and Rolf Langille's hired me to do some furniture refinishing."

"More lies," he says.

His eyes have gone empty. He straightens. He's still three inches taller than me. He walks toward me, slowly. I can't help it—I flinch.

He looks smug. Reaching out, he takes the collar of my T-shirt in his fist and tightens it around my neck.

No one should ask you to run a second marathon right after you ran the first one.

I seize his wrist, twist it hard enough to wrench his arm, knee him in the gut, then throw my weight at him. Let go, and watch him crash into a chair.

No enjoyment this time. Only shame, because it was so easy.

I say hoarsely, "Next time you lay a finger on Cassie or me, we're out of here. Straight to the cops."

Finally, I mean it.

I can't bear to be in the same room with him. I go upstairs, strip off my clothes, and stand under the shower for a long time, trying to wash it all away.

12.6 ["the end is the beginning ..." Japanese *koan* composed by Brickson MacAvoy]

A LESSON'S scheduled with Docker at four forty-five. I walk into the dojo in my bare feet; wincing, I bow at the old guy. Should have bowed at Floyd when he was tossing those logs on the grass. Never thought of it.

Reflected in the mirrors, Docker walks into the room. His eyes narrow. "What's up?" he says.

"Can I sit down?"

"Looks like you should be lying down."

He kneels beside me, the way I've seen him kneel when he's meditating. I fumble for words—pick them up, look at them, lay them down again.

"You've been fighting," Docker says. No expression in his voice. I nod. "Who with?"

"Floyd."

"Ah."

"I won. I guess."

"You don't look too happy."

I pick at the seam of my sweatpants. "Will I grow up like Floyd? He took up boxing, used it against me. Is that what I'll do with karate? If I ever have a kid."

"You planning to hang in with karate?"

"I *liked* hitting him! The look on his face when I kicked him ... playing with him as he got more and more tired."

"So after he fell down—I assume that's what happened— what did you do? Stand over him and gloat? Rub his nose in it?"

"I threw up."

"You'll be okay, Brick. After all, I've got three or four more years to drill those five principles into you."

"I don't think he'll quit. Even though I've threatened to set the cops on him."

"I think I'll pay a visit to your father," Docker says. "Make it clear to him I know what's going on, and that the whole world will know if he ever touches you again."

"You can't do that!"

"Brick, our aim is to stop your father beating you, without involving police, social workers, and foster homes. So he needs to know the problem's gone beyond the four walls of his house."

Docker hasn't raised his voice and his expression is, as usual, impassive. He's ten times the man Floyd will ever be, and he's on my side. I let this sink in.

Someday I'll ask him what happened to his wife and daughter.

"If you ever need it, the key to my back door is under the rock by the garage," he says. "It wouldn't be a bad idea for you to tell Rolf and Marigold about Floyd ... that way, you and Cassie have another place to go."

"I'm scared Rolf would go straight to the cops."

"You tell him to talk to me first."

Now that would be worth seeing—a standoff between Rolf and Docker. "He's gonna teach me stuff about woodworking."

"Talk to him. He'd understand."

"The karate you taught me ..." My voice trails off. I don't even know what I'm trying to say. How can I explain it's gone way beyond blocks and kicks?

"It'll be easier next time to hold Floyd off." Docker's eyes bore into mine. "And you know what I said. First time I hear of you using karate to start a fight or bully someone, you're out."

The lightbulb clicks on. "You knew all along that I bully kids."

"I'd heard rumors. But my gut kept telling me there was more to you than that."

"I'm almost sure my bullying days are done," I say.

"Good."

I manage something close to a smile. "I told Rolf I quit. You and him both on my case? No thanks."

Docker puts a hand on my knee and for once I'm okay with it. "People who don't know any better make fun of folktales and fairy stories. But the monster—the giant—is real. You took him on today, and you won. I'm proud of you."

"Thanks," I mumble, and pick at the seam some more. "And thanks for hanging in with me, Docker."

"My pleasure."

He means it. "I don't think I can handle a lesson today."

"Day off." He hauls me to my feet, smiling at me. All these people whose eyes know how to smile.

"I'll drive you to the beach," Docker says. "Why don't you buy yourself an ice cream, then sit on the wharf and eat it ... when you're done, you can call me and I'll drive you home. We'll have our regular lesson Friday."

Five minutes later I'm standing on the sidewalk near the ice cream stand. I feel a hundred years old, every bone in my body aching. The air is cooler here, the waves *shushing* on the sand, and suddenly I know what I'm going to do.

The Laughing Loon is open. I walk inside. No air-conditioning, but the windows are up, old-fashioned windows with small panes. There are rows of shelves jam-packed with books, the covers all the colors of the rainbow. Two overstuffed armchairs sit in an alcove just begging you to settle your butt and browse. Music is playing in the background. More of that classical stuff.

Glenn comes around the corner, Igor trailing him. "Hey, Brick."

No smile. You can't win 'em all.

Could be Mr. Semple's changed his mind about the freebie. "I ... I was just passing by."

"Igor's discovered he likes lettuce," Glenn says.

"Oh." Is he kidding? No, he's not.

"Dad was saying the other day you never came to pick out your book. He's in the stockroom. I'll get him."

If I come here again, I should bring a head of romaine. Or a Caesar salad. I bet Igor would like croutons.

I look around some more. History, Biography, Sports, Nature ... where will I begin?

Mr. Semple's walking toward me, beaming, one hand out-stretched. Same corduroy shorts. "Good to see you, Brick."

He squeezes my hand. Pain shoots up my wrist. He says, "Any book you want. Hardcovers, coffee-table book, whatever you'd like. Take your time."

In the end, I narrow it down to three: a book about a long stone wall this British guy designed in a park on the Hudson River; an encyclopedia of running; and a book about greyhounds.

I sit in one of the armchairs and leaf through them. Glenn and his dad are unpacking boxes of paperbacks, chatting back and forth. No room that I can see for any more books. Guess I should take the thickest.

The book about the wall wins out. I write down the titles of the other two in case they're available at the library. Or I could ask Mr. Semple to lay them aside, and pay for them later out of the stash.

Between the armchair and the cash register, there's a rack of cards. A photograph catches my eye. A girl on the beach, tossing a ball to a dog that's leaping in the air to catch it. *Joy* isn't a word I use much.

I'll send the card to Kendra. Just to say hello.

I can't see me and Cassie running away to Toronto, not when

I have friends right here on Hilchey River Road. But it would be nice to keep in touch with Kendra.

Mr. Semple takes cash for the card and puts the book in a bag. "Excellent choice. The artist's a fascinating man. Don't let those walls fool you—he's obsessed with the ephemeral. If you're interested, I can lend you some of his other books."

Ephemeral as sunlight through a hawk's feathers? "I'd like that. Thanks."

Through the open doors I can see the deck, with its wooden tables and canvas umbrellas. People are sitting out there, relaxing. I say, Joe Cool, "I guess I'll go outside and have a coffee."

I choose a table where I can see the ocean and order iced coffee with a cinnamon bun, as if I do this every day. Which is when I have a brainwave. I'll bring Tully here for our first date. Anyone can go to Tim Hortons. But the deck of The Laughing Loon has a touch of class.

Tully Langille has class.

The iced coffee slides down easy, and the bun is fresh.

My knuckles still hurt.

Beaver Lake ... Blazer, Sunfire, Cavalier, and Camaro ... chords coaxed from an old guitar and water lilies floating on a turquoise pond ... He didn't hit me the day I fumbled the ball for the fourth time. He never locked me in the dark and his belt stayed around his waist.

Am I supposed to feel grateful?

I look down at the plate. It's empty—I didn't even taste the last of the cinnamon bun.

I'll order another one.

Waves splash on the sand. The beach is a long, smooth curve, like the Buddha's robe. Against the sky, the horizon is as clean as the edge of a page.

I push the empty plate aside and open the book.

[author's note]

IF YOU'RE ever fortunate enough to travel the length of Nova Scotia's Eastern Shore, you won't pass through Hilchey Bay; it, and its residents, exist only in my imagination.

Cassie's favorite picture book is *That Stripy Cat*, written by Norene Smiley and illustrated by Tara Anderson, published by Fitzhenry & Whiteside.

The Dr. Seuss books that Cassie likes are *Horton Hatches the Egg*, *Horton Hears a Who!*, *Oh, the Places You'll Go!*, and *The Cat in the Hat*, all published by Random House.

The book Brick chose from The Laughing Loon is *Wall*, by Andy Goldsworthy, published by Harry N. Abrams.

Open: An Autobiography, by Andre Agassi, published by Alfred A. Knopf, is one of the titles that Brick takes out of the library.

Docker loaned Brick *The Shotokan Karate Bible: Beginner to Black Belt*, by Ashley P. Martin, published by Firefly Books.

The DVD that Brick and Cassie watch is called *AC/DC No Bull*, Elektra Entertainment Group.

Visit Jill's website at www.jillmaclean.com

[acknowledgements]

THIS BOOK needed considerable help along the way. My warm
thanks are extended to:

Barbara Markovits, who read a very early version of *Home Truths*, and
whose encouragement and insights were, as always, invaluable.

Mary Jo Anderson, whose suggestions later in the editing process
were informed by her ever-present intelligence and emotional
acuity—and by our long friendship.

My editor, **Ann Featherstone**, for how could this book have been
published without her? Right away she saw the problems with
an early draft, and we went from there—all the way to the
deadline. Keep that sense of humor!

Gail Winskill, for her continuing belief in my writing, and her
hard work on my behalf.

Sensei Tony Tam, 7th Dan, of the Dal Karate Club in Halifax,
who allowed me to observe several beginner classes. He kindly
undertook to read the pages of the manuscript that involved
karate, and to give me his feedback. Any errors are my own.

   He also granted permission to quote the dojo *kun*, the five
principles of Master Gichin Funakoshi.

John Doherty, of Pro Cycle, Dartmouth NS, for his help with the technical aspects of driving an ATV.

My family, **Dodie**, **Colin**, and **Stuart MacLean**, who answered questions ranging from hard rock to hoodies. Special thanks to Stuart and Colin for demonstrating self-defence tactics on the living-room floor. And thanks to **John Strowbridge** for help with Johnny Cash.

Anne MacLean, for last-minute editorial advice about the vernacular of Nova Scotians, and for friendship.

The Abbey Girls, who first heard me read aloud from *Home Truths*.

    I am very grateful for financial support, during the writing of *Home Truths*, from the Province of Nova Scotia through the Grants to Individuals Program of the Department of Tourism, Culture & Heritage.

    I am equally grateful to the Grants to Professional Writers Program of the Canada Council for the Arts. The money I received supported the lengthy process of editing *Home Truths*.